Praise for _Mayhem & De..._

'Enthralling. Dark and d[...]
magical stories defy easy d[...]
lessly combines the seasoned [...]
cholic preoccupation of the [...] ....ye of
a cinematographer. This is pr[...] ...ulsates, her stories are so
visceral you can hear their beating heart. Angela Carter for the
millennial generation.'
– Meena Kandasamy, author of _When I Hit You_

'A mature collection of dark and unnerving gems.'
– Ever Dundas, author of _Goblin_

Praise for Helen McClory
'McClory is clearly one of the best new writers to have emerged
in Scotland in the last few years…' – _The Herald_

Praise for _On the Edges of Vision_
WINNER: Saltire Society First Book of the Year Award, 2015

'Free from the debut trope of self-reference and loosely-
disguised autobiography, McClory engages in a kind of inquis-
itive modern mythmaking. Such macabre turns bring to mind
the terror of Ann Radcliffe or poetic justice of Roald Dahl.
One flesh-eating picnic scene, in particular, evokes Dahl's 'Lamb
to the Slaughter', but moreishly fresh in its own sense.' – _Gutter_

Praise for _Flesh of the Peach_
'Wonderful on the sentence level… If you are looking for a
Scottish debut with teeth, this is it.' – _Big Issue_

'Bold and unflinching, McClory's debut novel is _A Girl Is a
Half-Formed Thing_ meets _Inside Llewyn Davis_: a brutal, clear-eyed
study of a failing artist that shatters our expectations of what a
woman should be.' – Kirsty Logan, author of _The Gracekeepers_

MAYHEM & DEATH

HELEN McCLORY

Published by 404 Ink
www.404ink.com
@404ink

ISBN: 9781912489022
ebook: 9781912489039

Cover: ELEMdesign
Editor: Robbie Guillory

Printed and bound in Great Britain
by Clays Ltd, St Ives plc

1

CONTENTS

Stories have appeared in the following places:

Barrelhouse – 'Overwinternight'

The Bohemyth – 'What Can Be Endured May Yet Be Unbearable'

Blunderbuss – 'The Romantic Comedy' and 'The Expectation of a Job Well Done'

Denver Quarterly 51.4 – 'I was at last a romantic comedy about corruption and decay'

Gorse No. 5 – 'Museum Piece', 'Ritual Stitches, Good Red Wounds and 'Nostalgia Tremens' as 'Triptych'

Gutter No. 15 – 'The Beautiful Birds of the Aftermath'

Joyland – 'Souterrain'

Monkeybicycle – 'A Coven of Two'

Queen Mob's Teahouse – 'Six Places Where You Have Spoken'

Southword – 'Automaton Town'

Visual Verse (lead piece) – 'This Land'

The Wild Hunt – 'Lore' and 'Stick to Me, Peel from Me'

Wigleaf – 'The Companion'

Winter Tangerine – 'The Language of Heaven'

Also by Helen McClory:

Flesh of the Peach
On the Edges of Vision

For the lonely

SOUTERRAIN

It was high morning on a bright day in late March, the kind of
day when the earth begins to release scents it has kept pursed
all winter long. Up in one of the red sandstone tenements a
woman was touching the cushions of the window-seat in an
otherwise empty room. Frances: a study in sallow blotches
against white, puffy, slept-in skin, pale hair knotted at the nape
of her neck, a jumper tucked in heavy black folds into a red
skirt, under which rumpled winter tights, no shoes. She was at
that moment kneeling on the hardwood floor. Powered by the
purity of the sunlight on that late March day, she was not praying
but attempting to clean. Under one cushion of the window seat
she discovered a small, stiff, brass handle. Frances tugged on the
handle, and up came the wooden lid on a secret cache of her
daughter's things: up came a scuffed tin containing a lighter,
rollups, three squashed filters and a wiry clump of tobacco. She
sniffed – just tobacco, fine. Up came an old glasses case, the
one her daughter had told Frances she had lost – this was years
ago, when she was still in school. Other shifting debris, none of
which struck Frances as more than dimly poignant, until she
pulled up from the bottom of the cubby the black ledger.

The black ledger said "encase me in gold" in gold glitter on
the front cover, and Frances, running her fingers over the letters,
supposed they must be from a song lyric her daughter had
found. She opened the book and the spine of it creaked, and
Frances ran her fingers down the inner leaf. *Mayhem & Death*,
it said in a serious font, and underneath that, *A Nightmare Chap*,

1

lettering this time a black scrawl, marked over and over again in the same lines, until a groove had formed. Frances, repelled at first by the naked angstyness of the main title, tried mulling over all the meanings of 'chap': an old fashioned word for a man. To knock. To split or crack. A small book. It was, she thought, silly, the wrong word, something Madeleine would have picked.

She licked her finger and turned to the first page. There was a crabbed list in one corner with dates next to each. She looked at the first. 7th of November, 1999. That was the day Madeleine had started primary school. Later than everyone else because of that strange sickness that had for the early part of the term kept her body sunk in fever. The teachers said she would always be a little behind the other children, the doctors said she might even have been damaged by the sickness, a lasting damage. Madeleine's father had put on his grave-and-knowing act, but Frances would not take her daughter out and have her wait at home until the next class started, growing bored and tetchy. Madeleine, she argued, belonged with her peers. Even as Madeleine was called in to the head teacher's, repeatedly, for kicking students, for crying, for getting confused and loud when her spelling was corrected, for making strange drawings and gifting them to other children like an omen of their futures, for telling lies – as if a child of that age had anything worth lying about or worth punishing for lying about – for never being *good*, according to the fussy standards her teachers and peers had all somehow come to agreement upon.

And yes, because of this rough start, her daughter had always been a little behind, awkward. Frances had waited, first unconcerned and then impatient, then resigned, for the static to disperse from her daughter's personality; the obscuring details of herself that got between her and other people. But it never had gone away.

Frances got up stiffly and moved to the kitchen. She filled the kettle, she watched the kettle boil, she poured herself a tea. Too weak to stream in as it would in the summer, the sunlight hung suspended in front of the tall window, held back from her by the thin glass of the pane. The tea turned the hot water reddish-brown, the milk, added with care, turned it the colour of a cat Frances had once seen sleeping on a doorstep in a provincial French town. Frances sat herself at the kitchen table with the book and looked upwards at the crimson bed sheet and pillow slip drying on the airing beam overhead. After the list of dates, there were drawings of sea animals over the first few, wordless pages, fantastic creatures with giant eyes, backwards pointing teeth, and long tentacles. Recognisable as subaquatic beasties, boneless and sprawling their soft bodies outwards across the blankness. It was all a bit beyond Frances, but her daughter always loved the ocean. And that love, with its attentiveness and autodictatic seriousness, was what redeemed Madeleine, made her a worthwhile creation.

The dates corresponded with stories. She opened the book at the first date (page 6). The story there was a retelling of a dream, she thought, of darkness all around and a terrible pressure. It did not seem like something a child of that age could have dreamed, or even if so, articulated in the words in which it was written. But the form of the writing, familiar as Madeleine's, was childish enough that it looked as if it had been written at the time proclaimed. Steam came off Frances' cup and travelled in a fine faint skein up towards the ceiling. Frances tugged at the neck of her jumper, then at her neck itself. After she had finished the story, she did not know how to feel. She couldn't imagine her daughter writing it. Madeleine, who was, outside her one burning interest, discomforting but not in any way precocious, and in her schoolwork nothing more than lax, blissfully uncaring of deadline, Madeleine who was a shrug personified. A shrug and an indignant curse, maybe. But hadn't Madeleine used to like films, noir films, thrillers with the kind of atmosphere of this story? If nothing close to the surrealist air. *Mayhem & Death*. Perhaps it hadn't been right to show her such films when she was so young, but it had been the one thing they enjoyed together. They had watched films, every night, Frances' choices. Madeleine with toast, and coconut oil cheese melted over apple slices, lying full out on the white imitation sheepskin throw-rug, in utterly engaged consideration of what she was watching. *You know you can't swim that deep, no human could survive it.* Madeleine's dog-faced slippers kicking up and down. Her rejection of failure to communicate what was true, even when she knew it was for the purposes of fiction, it had to have truth in it, or be a waste. Her long glossy hair cutting over her shoulders. *There'd be bubbles in your blood, and you'd choke to death on blood in your lungs. I want to put something else on.* And the iron hishing as Frances sprayed a school shirt with scented water, performing a delicate perfuming she had never known growing up and that still felt like a ritual to do, and asking, off-hand, do you have any homework for tomorrow? And Madeleine sitting up and scowling. Then the arguments that always followed, and crying, and the days following tarred with her sullenness. Madeleine was like that, like a storm cloud poured into the shape of a girl, able to make a whole room feel the tortured static of her moods. She wasn't unaware of it, either. God, Frances hated her. Had hated her.

Frances rubbed her forehead, and hurriedly turned the page.

※

Frances was out walking towards Queen Street station with her bulging cotton shopping bag leaning into her side and too many folk going up and down the street. She had decided because she had no commitments she might as well take a train somewhere. Mallaig, as it turned out, about five-and-a-quarter hours distant from her life. She wanted to think fresh things, nourishing thoughts. However flaky that sounded in her own head – at least, the thought would go nowhere else. After all the waiting, the phone call, the letters, the interviews and the silence that followed, there remained the need to pull herself free, the impulse to move at least physically forward, even if in actuality she had not one thing in her life that held her in place.

Frances sat in her seat and, feeling ridiculous, took a selfie with the vivid soak of Garelochhead behind her, the mountains misted and hefty like they would never die. But even a mountain dies. Think of all the mountains that must have, before apes walked. Or during the ice age, when the white came down and levelled them, when the slow rivers of ice tore at their sides. Think of them, shifted of their green tonnes and tonnes of soil, rock, plant, squealing braying animals, shivering, falls and breakage and rockfall, silence, steady patters on the ground, someone coming at them with explosives, eating away at their bodies for commerce of ores and quarrystone. We are all just barely holding on, she told herself, looking at her face on her phone, always more asymmetrical, frailer, than in mirrors. Permitting herself a smile that, for god's sake, could look that pitiful.

She had a small tray table, and the possibility of a cup of bad coffee brought to her from down the aisle, and until it came, she leaned her elbows on the table and rested her head on the trembling window. The country gave the impression of crooked rowans and what else, white bark and pale green lichens prickling from branches the further north the train crept. There was Rannoch Moor with its waters shining silver. There was a whole other country in this country, grasses trembling in the winds, great big eroding lonely rocks, if you just kept going.

※

In Mallaig, Frances walked from the dead-ending train station to the wide ferry port. At some point she had gone into a little white building and come out carrying a plastic bag with smoked mackerel in it. Mallaig. It was the kind of town where the sea is always grey and the swells of it flecked with drizzle. It was where she belonged, yes, but there was nowhere she could think to find a place to stay.

She passed time standing between a wedge of white lines, watching the white and red hulk of a ferry shoulder across the waters. Ferry workers appeared and their yells sent her in retreat. There was a small guest house on Lovat Terrace, suggested a man in the lifeboat shop, try there. And tomorrow? And tomorrow, Frances thought.

The room was papered with magnolia wallpaper over woodchip, the bed had a rough blanket tightly bound over it. There was no tea to be had, so Frances drank a glass of water and picked the oily meat from the mackerel's almost clear bones, putting the bones and the packet into the bag it had come in and hanging this on the doorknob. She opened a window for the air. The view was suburban, though two streets or so to the right, the grey abyss swung under the white sky until, by degrees, it swung under the navy blue sky, its edges dissolved, and the lights of the houses went on, and Frances, tired of looking, lay down to sleep early with her smoked fish stinking fingers making fists at her sides.

In the early morning the seagulls shrieked into her dreams, and she too had a nightmare. Though in actuality more of a daydream: she lay awake, stroking her hair, thinking out the sequence of events and unable to make herself stop.

It began with Frances taking a long walk along the top of a windblown cliff. The sea was making a noise like the salt in it was hardening into crystals and these crystals were sharp, chipping away at the foot of the cliff. Onwards Frances went down a path that led her into some gorse bushes, bright with yellow flowers that in real life smelled to her like suncream smeared on chilled butter, though here they smelled of nothing, their scent transfigured into intensity of colour. The gorse, in explosive yellow, was mature, with thick branches reaching very high, or else she was smaller, and she lost sight of the cliff, or was in a different place without the cliff, because she realised she could no longer hear the wind or the salt-sharded sea, but where in most dreams placelessness or a sudden change is quickly accepted, here she became distressed, and wandered further into the spines of the gorse, becoming trapped in this hedge maze, this labyrinth silent and scentless and far too yellow to be borne. The dream-self saw no path through which there might be a centre, no clue to a way outside, back to the place where she had begun. But nothing, either, was chasing her, and the sun was warm, and the petals between the spines were delicate, and nothing less than beautiful, though it made her wince to think of such an unruly thicket of plants in that flaky term, beautiful. She took nothing from its beauty as reassurance: it was the absence of any real fear to the scene which Frances held on to when these insistent, intrusive thoughts finally let her go.

§

The air was painfully cold and wet on Frances' face: if she looked towards the horizon, she could pretend she only wanted what was there, the island, emerging in dusky purples, where the ferry would dock. There was a tall man in a green waxed jacket on the red deck, talking to a companion, a short mousy woman in a blue coat. She could want that – but the couple were parting, the companion was moving off. They did not know each other, or they did, and the woman was sent to fetch a coffee, and there she went away clumsily, pushing herself through the oval door to the stairwell. Down into the bowels where the canteen was.

"Fantastic day, isn't it?" the tall man was saying, arms pinned as he gripped the white guardrail. Frances gave herself two options. She chose the latter, and turned stonily towards the swells, going after that specific power to be had, smaller than a grain of sand, in refusing to capitulate to a greeting from a stranger. This power embeds itself under their skin, an unscratchable itch and you've put it there, and if you have managed it once successfully with no rancour on either side, then later you may allow this act to be repeated, the act of keeping yourself to yourself, and others accepting your actions.

"Fantastic, right?" said the man. "Right…" he clapped

his hands and looked as Frances had feared he would. She sighed and pulled out her phone. A reminder that she had an appointment at two o'clock with her grief councillor. In Glasgow, however many hundreds of miles away. She brought up a selfie of Madeleine at her last training session before launch day, which Frances had not attended, or been invited to attend. Her daughter was looking bold in her uniform, casual though it was – blue polo-neck with a logo like she worked at a golf resort instead of a sociological and marine research station. Behind Madeleine, hulking machinery covered in rivets took up space to a mysterious purpose, but with kinship, distantly, to the boat Frances was now on.

"This is my daughter, Madeleine," Frances said, holding up the phone.

"Oh, off to see her then?" The man in the wax jacket seemed unbreakably earnest as he looked at the photograph.

"Yes, I suppose so," said Frances.

"Does she live on Skye, or is she just doing a course–"

Again, Frances had two options before her.

"Oh no, she doesn't live on the island. She doesn't live on land at all, actually. She's dead, they tell me. But I don't know if you can be alive or dead, where she is. There's no stone, no grave I can visit, though there's talk that they'll make the under-water station a kind of memorial, but how that counts as a grave if you can't visit it I don't know. There's an effort ongoing for retrieval of the bodies from some of the other families. They've got the money, the lawyers, I suppose. The energy."

After a time, the mousy companion came back, holding plastic cups. The tall man was by then sitting in a red bucket chair in a row of red bucket chairs planted on the red deck below the ferry's white flank, his back turned to Frances, peering at a guide book to the best whisky distilleries in the whole of the country, the truly unmissable ones.

Mayhem & Death

❦

Frances was in the spongy, spiky interior of the island, walking along a gritty and uneven path blotted by puddles. She had heard there was a waterfall, but having seen it and been unimpressed, she had continued along between the recently-planted sapling pines in their beige plastic tubes, taking in all the shades of brown the unsprung spring countryside had to offer. One day, she thought, raising her hood as it began to smirr again, I'll live in places not riddled with the damp. Somewhere clean, where the foliage snaps off at the beginning of November and is covered in snow until April, nothing like this dying into spore-y tangle and just staying there. Summers would be scorching hot: she would walk out on summer days, all day she'd walk and at the end of the day she would sleep well with a lightly burnt face and a head full of vistas of blue sky and hills. She'd never been anywhere other than here, the mainland and some of the outer-lying islands, and Ireland once – no use expecting drier days there. And there were the two trips to France, the flatter parts, and where she could really only remember the tawny cat sleeping on a step, and some minutes spent staring at a water meadow from the car as her and her ex butted heads about a missed turning and certain domestic inadequacies. Right now, in the near-invisible rain, Frances couldn't picture what a dry landscape would even look like. Madeleine would have rolled her eyes and pulled up something on her phone to show me, Frances thought. But no, she wouldn't have. Madeleine had moved away. Madeleine no longer loved her enough to stay above the sea, above the fantastic disaster which had claimed her.

Frances kept walking on for a time until her nose began to run and she stopped, looked at the beleaguered hillocks, breathed out, turned and walked through increasing drizzle the eight or so kilometres back to her rental car. She was staying in a white-washed inn with a great fire in the fireplace that looked like it had been snapping and licking the grate since 1745. She sat by the fire and had a whisky and stared into the pale flames. A few tables over, a group of hikers were playing scrabble. They all had good faces; high cheekbones, skin red and raw from the outdoors, with bright eyes and frizzy hair tied back, even the men. Frances watched them, and felt herself thaw. The men young, but weathered. The women acute, not smiling but with great purpose in their movements, good speckled woollen jumpers in greens and navy, boots that had taken them tramping round corries and scampering up all the sharp arêtes the mountains had to offer. It was not good, this type of thaw in her. She might start thinking of Madeleine again, in public. Better maybe she'd stayed in Glasgow. In the flat, forcing herself to sit it out, sit out the walls and the pace of one mouldering, pinched day and another, and another. Frances focused on the bottom of her whisky glass, and the swilling golds everywhere there, and the cheap burgundy carpet underfoot, the shadowy antlers over the fireplace, the black book with the gold glitter writing tucked safely in her bag. She thought of how there is no such thing as 'safe'. Eventually she decided to go to her room before the scrabble players could be done, so she could know they were there in the bar where she had left them, where they were living and wholesome, even if it was not possible to be like them.

In her room she washed her face and brushed her cold ash-yellow hair. In her room she was in her room, as much as she could manage.

※

Mayhem & Death. Why had she written it? thought Frances, running her thumbnail down her daughter's handwriting. Madeleine had never known either, not at least as far as Frances was aware, though she couldn't discount there might have been secrets, suffering, wounds that her daughter had seen or experienced and kept, in shame, to herself. It's better never to have children, she thought. Larkin, that poem – Madeleine had been reading Larkin for school, more than a decade and a half ago, and certain things must have stuck. There was in some of his poems something she recognised and ached for, and knew her daughter had too. Just as when they had watched *Inside Llewyn Davis* together. A crisp, cold, nihilism, bracing as winter, and just as reassuring. Frances thought she needed those sorts of deep white winters, almost gone from this country, because of their shape, their *old* feeling. Winters are older by a long way than springs. Then life is older than death, she thought, because the latter needs the first. That's it. Life is the first thing out of the brace of winter, tiny and pulpy, gasping – and a close second, death. And far, far after that, the grass is growing, things are blooming sickly-scented and everything is abundant, falling to mush with abundance, but by then it's already too much of an afterthought, a soppy, almost but not entirely false reassurance from life of life's success, that ought to be understood as such, in the face of the second of all things. Madeleine hadn't quite got to that point of understanding, hadn't quite made it beyond a teenager's understanding of death as a simple dramatic *boom*, drop to the floor, without this sense of recursive, also-ran contradiction and self-deception. But, thought Frances, I'm only up to her dreams and thoughts from when she was what, fourteen? Nothing so far had proved illuminating, about Madeleine herself or anything outside of Madeleine. *How much have I missed of her?* Frances thought. Probably not much, not the things I want to know. *What age, even, was she when she died? Was she safe?* She screwed up her eyes then looked out of the window in her room at the road and the loch some way back from it, across the sodden, dead, bog land. Frances, you are still going, she thought. You are going to go to the place where it all stops, and then pass through that gate, and all this will have clarity. You will just have to keep going until it does. Or it doesn't.

Frances had the map open on one of the tables. It was an old map, but roads wouldn't change much around here, she thought, and in any case, what she was looking for was a sight older. Her finger traced a line in pencil to a small x under the words Kilvaxter souterrain. She thought: is that a bit much, to go down into a low house, where the dead might be thought to dance, or the fairies? She scowled at herself, both the indulgent self, and the self that threw up restrictions.

Well, something a little less obvious?

Like talking to someone?

No, but to be a woman on her own in her grief was to be the recipient of the thickest, tar-like pity from anyone about who wasn't immediately repulsed: you could want that pity, sometimes, but it would leave her weaker. She skipped most sessions; no one ever seemed to mind. None of the other parents had written back to her when she emailed about the incident that had taken their children too. She would – she would do as she had been doing. You are an inch closer to the dead at this time, she told herself, and not to take advantage would be boring.

Frances, though knowing herself at all turns constrained by the expectations of those around her, stranger and familiar alike, and never before wanting to upset anyone unduly by the force of her personality knocking ripples across someone else's day, had never wanted to be without the option to, sometimes and without fuss, tear the whole world fucking down. Even having a child – which, yes, she had resented – had not snuffed these feelings entirely. For a long time she had been content to feel the pulse of that desire without acting upon it, the tension was enough. Now grief made it permissible, occasionally, for her to appraise a situation and act beyond the normal acceptable standard, but not too much, too loudly, or too long. Blanking on greetings, missing appointments, wandering off out of her life, all this was fine. But what good was any of it, the freedom to be here or there, a selfish arsehole here or a selfish arsehole there? Frances pushed her hands down on the table top until her finger tips were pale: how better life would be if instead, in pushing, the table would give in, gently letting her slip her fingers through the layer of polish, through grain of the wood. She felt someone watching her. It was a young man with a beard, off through a doorway, seated at the bar, which should have been shut (it was a Sunday morning) but was glowing merrily, sunlight trapped and dancing in the whisky bottles, even the cheap American stuff. The man at the bar raised his glass to her. Frances ducked her head away. And then softened: he was a calm looking sort, one of the hikers from the day before – there was his green woollen jumper, wrapped around his waist like a little boy would do. You never knew what might turn out to be permissible, even cheering to other people, that you had spent your life withholding from yourself. Ach well, she said to herself, the souterrain then, while we have the light. And before her eyes, a glitter as off wet stone.

❦

A small patch of bog myrtle was thrashing about and flattening itself and springing up again. Surrounding the patch, wastes of dank brown grasses and the heather with its little dry florets were doing the same on a smaller scale and dictated by the physics and wiriness of their own materials. Frances held her pale hair to her head so that it would not blow into her eyes, and pressed on. She came to the stone hole which was the entrance to the souterrain. It was small and low, not much to look at, not much to describe to herself, except that it made her vaguely dizzy to stare into it. She crouched down and pulled a torch out of her bag. Moorland wind in uninterrupted force screamed in her ears but the hole was silent, and she could feel its silence and dark held there below better than a human fist can hold the silence and the dark, for this had been doing so far longer. All it was, for centuries, was a tunnel of several metres leading to a small chamber, and in the small chamber, if it was as they usually were, nothing discounting the gravel sprinkled for the visitor to tread on, the welcome of the tomb.

For a little while, standing above the souterrain, Frances brushed the lintel and the stone floor with the yellow light from her torch. She even descended once and touched the roof with her bent back. And then she thought of the young man at the bar. And thought between cold stone, underworld, liminal passages, femininity, graves, storage or a buried dwelling to what really, at the moment, drew her most urgently. The living. The fleshly. The prickly. The cause. The tiles of scrabble scattered and picked up by people she did not know and never would speak to, and who would not like her and her great neediness if they did (Madeleine hadn't, had she?). The beat of her heart, which she could not hear over the silence of this open mouth. A fact which made her feel deeply angry and aggrieved with this place, above all other vexations. She pulled her daughter's book out of her bag and flicked the pages in agitation. Of course she was meant to bury it here, now that she had read it, or enough of it to see that Madeleine's dreams or her accounts of them had been dark ones, much as her teachers and her school peers had said, to drop it in the dark and leave it behind, like her daughter's body was in the dark even now, far below the surface of the world. Not to drop the book here would be a kind of failure to overcome her grief. But in whose eyes? Still holding *Mayhem and Death*, she turned and climbed out of the souterrain back into the moorland and raised her head, feeling spits of rain on her neck, and pulling her zipper up against them.

"Oh, fuck you," Frances said to the souterrain, flapping the book at it without bothering to look back.

She dropped off her cotton bag in the luggage rack and hesitated, holding her purse in hand. She could do with a drink. But there was the issue of intruders, blunderers, taking her seat when she was up, thieves taking her things, even the useless things that were in that bag, or else the train decoupling and going down extra tracks for reasons announced in some intercom babble she might miss. The walls of the train shuddered as the engine was turned on. Frances smiled. She briefly thought of the silent base underwater thousands of miles away where her daughter had gone, and in which all occupants, including her daughter, were now long held to be dead. And here she was, on a train, again! About to go somewhere, through the open-air countryside, where all around things were about to burst into life, grow fast, and whither, and drop dead. And Madeleine was not, because she already had. Frances left her place and walked down the narrow hall into the lounge carriage, and straight to the bar for a tiny bottle of vodka and a tiny bottle of tonic water and a modest-sized plastic cup in which to mix them, no ice already. She sat by the window of the drinking carriage, which wasn't hard to do, and ignored the people who had, like her, already begun filtering in, which was harder – she so very much wanted, in all her stubborn unlovedness, unloveableness, to love them. The train did not move, then the platform moved, then the train with great labour began to depart.

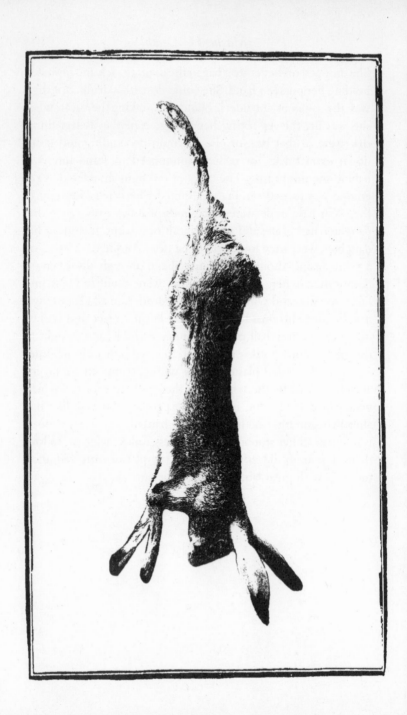

LORE

They killed the hare when the mist was on the early morning river. They had come upon her in an abutting field while crossing it silently out on a hunt. She lay in her form, resting, eyebright and whiskers quivering. Dew on the long and parted grass. One man whistled through his teeth. She did not move. Her nose moved. Someone cocked their gun.

The youngest held her body by the ears. Long creature, with great elegant legs and feet, fur the colour of clay. They tied her to the grouse pole, and brought her back with a double brace. The house was empty of the womenfolk when they returned. Outside, the trumpets of daffodils blared bright against an encroaching bank of smoke-white fog. Most of them thought nothing of it. The women were away at town, having piled into the Ford. The weather could change on a penny-spin. They brought the bounty to the large pantry, and strung up the birds, and laid the hare down on the table, beside the grapes and bread.

It was only much later, evening time, when a voice from the garden began to call. The men sat smoking at the fire, talking little, drinking brandy. At first it was distant. The sound of the wind passing through a low hedge, or a radio muffled in static. But there was no wind at all, and theirs the only room lit up, and the country road ran around them in the dark.

My wife, came the voice, *my wife is lost in the fog.*

My husband, came the voice, *my husband is lost in the fog.*

I have licked the moonlight from her fur. I have combed his long black ears. But now I can't find her.

The men sat, smoking and slurping at their drinks. Not one of them moved.

The voice came closer, louder. *My wife. My husband. Where are you?*

Somewhere a door opened, great locks sliding back.

The sound of soft footsteps. Doors opening.

Oh, my love lies on a table, eyes gone dim. A hole in his side and the blood out of her.

The voice was larger, larger now. Steps echoed through the hall.

Which beasts have done this? Where will the moon go now the hare is dead?

Tell me

Tell me

The voice was just outside. It boomed like the Spring sea. A masculine voice, a feminine one, flowing between the two. Close at hand came the sound of doorframes splintering under an immense pressure. Three stamped flagstones shattered with a bone-deep crack. The men leapt up and dragged the walnut table to bar the billiards room door. Some held it steady, while others cringed against the wall, or behind the milk-white settee. It had come. The walls thuddered, pounded.

Tell me

Tell me who has done this

Hearts like shrivelled fruits. Fists ready. Guns held tight.

Outside, the garden sat at peace. Fog resting on it. Stars above, glimmering like the dew.

One long shriek and a crashing, tearing sound. Hush.

A puttering engine behind a curve in the lane. Lights bounced closer. The car came to a steaming, ticking stop, and the women got out and stood. The sounds of evening had fallen away. The house was utterly still and dark.

They unsnibbed the door and went in, going from room to room, calling callooh. At last one reached the billiards room. She opened it without knocking. The men, crumpled on the settee or propped in stiff backed chairs, all rose at once and turned their heads. Raised their hands in greeting, they showed their spotted gums and began, all at once, to speak.

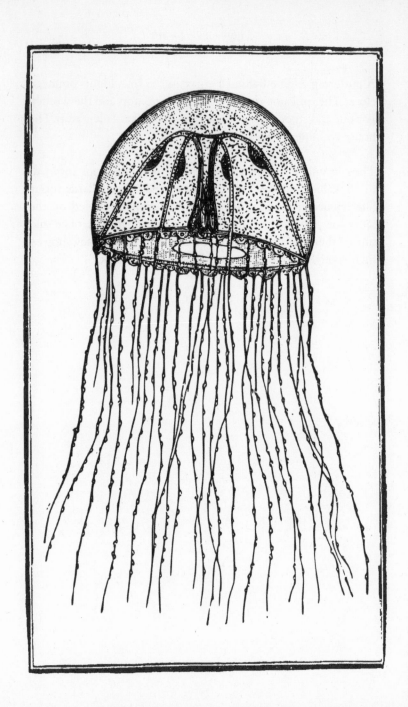

DISTINCTIVE
NATURAL PATTERNS

Cameras caught the team steeling themselves before they stepped off the scree and entered the wood. From there on they walked uphill, three men, hunkered in parkas, lugging kit. No dogs, no horses. They knew that our house was at the end of the straight white gravel trail, beyond the ridge. After the treeline it is always worse; the weather closes in. Navigation possible only with foreknowledge of the landscape, alacrity to the interlock of burns and fording points, scramble points, footholds, points above the fog, how long it will take to walk between each with a hand stretched out and the wolves behind. We waited, making ready to receive them.

Of course there are no wolves, not officially. Just as the crow blackout, too, is a fancy. A thousand crows passing ragged overhead, to drop into the wood and never be seen again. At this late stage of the Anthropocene there is no normal, neither for bird nor animal nor us. Hidden in one hanging valley a purple and white meadow of lowland orchids and damp sundew thrives despite the scour of the winds. The world is thin material up here, but beautiful. Often, in the afternoons, we will see a rainbow, broken in scraps as if sacked for parts and left limp on the wall of the sky.

When the team reached our house, its elegance surprised them. Our first predecessor was eccentric, we have been told, and wanted the architecture of her dreams, with curving overhangs, external, ringing metal stairs and bright colours abutting the concrete. It was our mother who painted it the rust-red it is now. Our mother, who lies on the leeward side, under a heap of stones in earth too shallow to bury any morsel bigger than a bird.

We stood to greet them on the viewing platform in our white, twinned, embroidered smocks. Come in, we said. Introduce yourselves, we said.

Jesse, Mark, Jun.

We brought down hot soup and blankets, had them sit to recover a while before we confirmed who we were. I am Maggie, she is Aretty, we were made to live forever. As in fact our mother had been too, as each predecessor had, each now dead of their own weariness, with the force our sort requires. There was once an animal called the immortal jellyfish, a type of creature that will never die. On injury or nearing cell collapse the immortal jellyfish reverts to a pre-adult form, the medusa, from which to build again. At least in body. Survival for such as us is default, and everything else a variable, a fight.

When we sent Jesse and Mark and Jun to their beds, we talked about them with something akin to affection. In their rucksacks we found packets in sealed foil, the usual heating kits and gas canisters, the tubes and the syringes. We put these things aside. I climbed the stairs to the guest rooms and looked in through the wall slot: they were sleeping now, or pretending to sleep. Arrety dispensed the sedative through the matching slot in the air duct. We make it easy. We have known the mess of blood and absent answers, and feelings whose names we do not know, but have the textures of copper, grease, sliding down our throats and lodging there.

Daylight came up on the mountain, spreading quick and cold, catching us out in the rock field in the shadow behind the house. There we had set each clean body in its afforded place. It is beautiful this world when the flags on the highest cairns flutter all in unison in the vigorous morning air. It is beautiful, I insist on it, though Arrety will sometimes disagree. We are, anyway, the same.

Sky burial in the first instance, then stones arranged on the remains. I gave the whistle, which Arrety has never learned to do. First the crows come up from the wood, whirling, rags that make the whole. After, the wolves in their paced slink, bowing yellow-eyed to my sister and myself. An order out of order. And all leaving us again as is natural when the work of their hunger is done.

SIX PLACES WHERE
YOU HAVE SPOKEN

In the French church, when it was taken outdoors for Easter. I don't remember the closest town, only the greenness, the fact it could be warm to sit out of doors. A china rabbit crouching in my palm. And your voice, hard like a pair of paint-spattered overalls, after mass was over, telling me to duck below a branch.

No I was mistaken. Reverbing branches come at you like a fierce message. Puncture says the skin. Little prints laugh indented and the lips raised. Blood sketch on the ground. I held in my teeth, but I hadn't been hit by you, not then.

I rolled my eyes at officials and smoked, getting lipstick prints on the filter. I wandered out on an adventure. I forgot my tidy life and lived it forgetfully. I shed the various names for grace. I fractured my fingers, I fell in with a faceless crowd. I spoke flatly, without qualities, pretending that was possible. There was a silence that was my being told.

In the house on the rock by the lake. I was told, if you need to tell someone, tell the sea. If you are far from the sea, a river will do: the words will make their way downstream eventually. If there's no river, not even a stream, at hand, go to the mountain. Don't ever tell the lake. Don't. But I drank whisky and I sat by lake and I told.

When the needle pushed in and out of my skin, point gleaming like a star. I need someone to tell me before I am hurt, I said, silently. I held a silent thing with a smushed face, and my blood. The nurse had hard, strong hands, and the outside world was fogged blue beyond the walls. The tattoo on my wrist was half a pockless moon. What do you think the difference is between good and safe? I asked myself. I winced, and the nurse looked up with his teeth and he said, not long now.

When that woman shamed my gentle boy, when that woman peeled him down to be laughed at in a room full of paper and guts. I wanted sanctuary for us both. I wanted you to tell me the river knows, the sea knows, and that the red years will suck the bruise. Lap says the wave. Death says my baby. I realised then that was all we ever say. For the first time like a saint I heard you say in your still, laconic voice, *oh honey, no.*

THE INCITING
INCIDENT

A nd here is the room: black beams in the ceiling, floor highly polished, baseboards recently washed, the large and handsome bed made up with sheets stretched tightly over the mattress. The eiderdown quilt in white with a red satin stitching, the windows large and with interior shutters pressed against the wall allowing light from outside, allowing too sight of the damp garden, with its large spring-growth yew hedges and drizzle-stained oaks. Off to one side is the writing desk, dainty, it might be said, with a row of books with leather and striped spines held up by their own attainment. A chair is pushed in neatly against the desk, with a blue cushion tied to its seat by blue ribbon in a knot that nothing but a needle could unpick. There are no rugs on the floor, rush or rag or otherwise.

If we talk about the room long enough, then we do not have to talk about it; do not have to discuss what he did (to her – we presume to *her*), do not have to attempt to parse the motivation behind his actions, murky as that might be as is a silt-laden river driving through low country like the country outside. If we may just indicate the room, and its aspect, layout and furnishings, its position on the third floor of the house, then we do not have to talk about her, expose her bluntly to our scrutinising gaze. We don't have to move on to record if she survived, or if not. And if she survived, we don't have to lay judgement on the way she managed this, or anything of how the community magnified and judged her portrayal of her own aftermath, what verdicts they made on her movements before and after the incident – night, no moon – there may be no need for any of those details, though the hunger for them might be irredeemable, now. But here, here is the room.

Here, in this room, let's be gentle, with our fists at our sides. In this room there is a wardrobe very large against the wall, seeming to conceal a secondary exit perhaps, in dark wood conveying weight enough to be a confessional or a covered sedan chair set at rest with the runners cut off, or any such place that hides a body in dire need to hold itself within an enclosed, darkened space that mutes and shields their activities, their emotions, their body and soul from being an open wound in the open wound of the world. It is perhaps *too much* to ask us to set aside our needs and visualise only a room, talk around the incident, make its shape obliquely, wring hands or let our eyes glaze over until there is a dog, too, belonging to the house. Something living, at last. Here we can picture as he appears snout-first around the door, a very large wolfhound with no collar and the usual sad expressive eyes like wet coals. Sad demonic eyes.

So now there is in this room, where something happened, at least a dog in it, climbing with his almost human-scaled limbs onto the bed, to inhabit it more fully the way a dog, and only sometimes a person, will do. Be thankful. A dog cannot hate us for our uninspected hungers. There's an admirablity in the kind of urgency a dog has that is in almost all ways different from our own.

A room can have disorder or stains in it. But this room does not, will not. All is in order, now. Let's take one last look, one long breath in and out. A room in a story cannot be a haunted room, unless the writer puts the ghosts in there, or the suggestion of ghosts into it. *They say the stain reappears. He was haunted the rest of his days. They say there is the reek of smoke around midnight. Everything she ever wrote he burned.* There is a white china vase of dried lavender on the desk against the wall. A ghost is the idea of a moral outcome for unjust acts or at least their possibility outwith the usual frames of justice. There might then be the suggestion of the concealing scent of lavender in the still air, or cedar from the wardrobe, but then, there might be nothing. The room has been recently aired, perhaps. The mistress' imagined dog whines and falls asleep. What have we been given, and what are we desperate, now, to take away? There is a certain mood, but to define it is to put it out. No: a bird flies across the window; there are swifts' nests tumorous in the eaves. There was a note on the desk, but it has been removed.

THIS LAND

This land's so full of spikes like you wouldn't believe. Saul broke earth this spring early and found rows of them growing like dragons' teeth under the thin soil.

"Come out, Alice," he yelled. "See this."

Then it was a lot of questions for me. Had I happened to drop them, while I was out walking so much?

I said, "Now where would I get a handful of spikes like these from?" They were two inches long, of a thin bright metal, no sign of rust. Much heavier than they looked. The blunt ends plain and the sharp ends enough to poke through a potato's eyes with no resistance. I know. I did it at the kitchen table, after Saul was done trying to get his answers from me. Potato with spikes through it. Looked like witchcraft, so I pulled the spike out and threw the tater quick on the fire.

He asked around the neighbours – each a half-hour drive away on the tractor – someone should know what the last lease-holders had been doing, if it was anything so strange. The neighbours said it was our land, our problem now. Saul tried to puzzle that one out a while.

"They seemed like good folks," he told me, "but they went cold when I mentioned the spikes. They wouldn't even take a look at them."

"All of them the same way?" I asked.

Saul looked to heaven, "Yes, all of them, like I said."

I was cleaning out the barn for the cattle coming. It was a good place, no need of repair. But in the back there was a shelf, and on the shelf I found the spikes, raised up. Free-standing like there were weights in the bottoms of each, but when I plucked one up, tried the same on the floor, I couldn't find the balance. I showed these spikes to Saul and he flung them off the edge of his property. Some of them got in the road, and I cleared them later in case they caused mischief with passing wheels.

Another time I found a fistful of spikes in a cornmeal sack we'd brought unopened to the house with us. I didn't show these to Saul. Soon every place I found to look I saw spikes. They were malicious things. I cut my hand on one, lifting up a dead mouse from the pantry. I looked closer: the mouse was studded with smaller spikes, shining brightly all down the length of its spine, sharp ends pushing out from the inside. I shuddered and disposed of the creature quick. If I was a fearing woman, I'd have left that day. Out on the fields Saul stood at rest with his pitchfork glinting, dusk coming on across the expanse. I felt a necklace of the spikes clitter heavily against my throat. I stood silent, staring and staring through that window, one hand resting on this weight.

AUTOMATON TOWN

They had bought the automaton town from a strange man in small offices in the city. They had bought the automaton town, and had it wrapped in soft cloth and transported by barge so as not to risk damage. When the barge came to the closest point to their home they sent men with a specially constructed pallet to lift the automaton town and walk it across the lawns and into the ballroom, where it filled nearly a quarter of the floor space. There may never be dancing again, thought the daughter of the house. But her father and her mother smiled, and directed that the key should be wound, and the automaton town shown.

They sat on plush chairs. Two servants were permitted to remain in the room, the key-winder (the butler's son, with his strong arms), and a maid, in case one of the ladies should need attending to. At first, nothing happened but a faint noise of cranking gears. Then, bit by bit, the town came to life. A pink-faced washerwoman appeared at a window, shaking a wooden sheet. A man in a white wig walked out of a doorway, gesturing with his pipe. A baker in his bakery sawed at a loaf of bread, in time to the swaying geraniums in the flowerpot outside. A woman in green shuffled down the street with a poodle, which began to bark. A small, tinny, but unmistakably poodle-like bark. The man in the small offices had said there were over four hundred 'players' in the town, and while it seemed preposterous at the time, it now made itself violently evident. Wooden figures streamed out of doors, or moved behind windows. It was impossible to make them all out, there were so many. Down a side street, a cart was upset, spilling apples as a horse reared in fright. High up in a tenement, a man with blocky fists punched a woman in a red apron in the jaw, and she stumbled backwards against a wall. The noises grew, a mesh of sounds that filled the ballroom. The daughter covered her ears, while her parents sat enraptured. Night came to the town. Revellers appeared. The pub lights came on, and frothy ales were poured. In the alley beside the church, a woman lifted her skirts and a man thrust an oversized coin into her hand. A brawl broke out in the market square. A man stabbed another man and removed his fob watch. A dog with a great mouth barked, until it too was stabbed and left on the wooden cobbles.

The daughter nudged her mother, only to be shrugged off. She tried to catch the eye of the maid, but the maid was looking down at the floor – was she, was she crying? The daughter felt her own face. It felt hard, numb. Plague came to the town, the doors to the city gates were barred. A man dragged the cart into the square, a cart loaded with white-painted corpses. They fell with a clatter into a hole in the stage floor. A group of women entered the church, which then split open, revealing them inside, pulling out the pews and smashing in the glass windows. The priest came out from the confessional, holding out his arms: the man from the other side of the confessional raised his fists and struck him to the flagstones.

The maid muffled her face to keep in her screaming. The father tutted, but did not look her way. The daughter attempted to rise and was restrained by her mother. The buildings of the town folded and reformed into new dimensions. Briefly a city like the cities of the day, modern, with a railway station and omnibuses. These sank under the stage flooring – next arose a solitary building, a great mansion surrounded with trees. Such detail – polished wooden apples swung from their branches, a tiny blackbird chirruped in the rose garden. There was the canal made of moving strips of glass. There the lush green lawn. And there, across the lawn, wooden men, carrying a pallet on which there was a shape wrapped in soft cloth. The mansion split open slowly. Rooms rotated to reveal intricate furniture – the plates, the painting of family likenesses, the grandfather clock (with working pendulum).

Panels from the bottom of the automaton town's stage flipped outwards and clicked down on the fine ballroom flooring. It has reached the second window now, the daughter thought. In the wooden mansion, the cooks were pressing dressed meat into oven mouths, were chopping onions by the window. A man in shirtsleeves was taking off his hat to speak to a finely-dressed girl at the foot of the stairs. He was walking up the stairs with the girl ahead of him, guiding her with his hand. They were entering a bedroom. In the bedroom without removing their clothes they jerked their wooden bodies together on the bed. They danced like pegs. A maid at the door bent to peer into the keyhole.

The father sat very still, and so did the mother.

The maid by the wall had stopped crying, and was now looking at the daughter, trying to signal something with her eyes. The daughter looked down at her stiff dress, and her small white hands.

Five figures entered a ballroom, and arranged themselves, three in the plush chairs, one by a wooden construction at the far end, the last by the wall. But, if one looked closely, they could see faces at the window looking in. Their mouths open, no, opening. Ratcheting open to the fullest extent. The daughter turned to the windows of the ballroom, but all she could see was the stillness outside.

Something had happened. A figure chirped, *wind the mechanism!* The automaton town had stopped. *Wind the mechanism!* The father ordered, *there will be more – look at those faces there!* But the butler's boy did not move.

The automaton town, of its own volition, began to roll again.

THE BEAUTIFUL BIRDS
OF THE AFTERMATH

For my Dad

From dawn, the birds were taken from their boxes and placed in a long row on the wall of the battery. Maree's job was to smooth out the feathers and check that all parts of the birds were still sturdily affixed. She had brought up a box of eyes and another of claws. The feathers were hard to get hold of; the town ordered in fresh skins and extras of the long filamentaries direct from Tasmania – these were expensive, but the budget allowed for the cost, and if there was insufficient money around, chapping door-to-door would do the job. Maree wasn't allowed to cut corners. Each bird had to look pristine, or else the problems would begin again.

Sixteen years ago, there had been a huge landslip off the mountain, a result of fracking, or the will of God, or the heavy rains that winter, depending on who you asked among the townsfolk or the local authority. In one morning the primary school had been buried along with the graveyard, the local supermarket. Parents out getting the shopping were killed at the same instant as their children a quarter of a mile away. Little ones, fretting over their times tables or running the beep test in the gym when first the windows then the seventies concrete walls on the northern side of the buildings all gave in to tonnages of oozing dark brown mud and shale fragments. The slip flowed on, crushing and upturning the world. The tide of mud had reached to the sea, then spilled over into it, like the contents of luggage tipping off the edge of a bed. The sound of the falling earth burst the eardrums of half the survivors.

The weather grew unusually dry about that time, and so the mud became dust, and blew about the place, sometimes hanging in a cloud so dark that the town seemed to live in the half-light of a partial eclipse. It was just as the last loads of dirt were being ferried and dumped into the sea that the bird appeared to Tobey Silks. Silks, a dull man otherwise and new-made widower, saw the bird appear in the dingy sky as he came to open his grocery shop. He said it had glided down from the roof, gentle like. It was the size of a partridge, plump bodied, with this great glorious long tail that fanned out, a bit like a peacock's, but whiter, and coiled at the tips. It stood on the bins near the bread pallets, and it cocked its head at him, and then flipped its tail feathers out – here Tobey would try to explain exactly how it had flipped them, spreading his fingers wide and putting it over his balding head. Like this, he'd say, but beautiful. Then it opened its mouth, and sang.

Tobey was deaf at that time, though he had since regained part of his hearing. But he knew it was singing, and he knew that it was the most wonderful sound in the world. The noise of a rainforest, full of sparks and crackling leaves and twirls of other bird and animal cries, and water bubbling downwards, and animals scouting in the water, and fish gaping and hovering in portions of light. That the birdsong came from the far past, a world without humans and human suffering. He talked about human suffering, inevitable as it is, put to the balm of this bird's song, and the possibility of it singing as a gift to heal them, all of them in this broken town. All this was a lot, coming from Tobey Silks.

It was he who bought the first stuffed Superb Lyrebird, and put it in the grocery window, first so that everyone could see what he meant, then as a charm.

A year later, the din of a second landslip hit the town on the same day and hour, and the third was exactly one year from that, and the fourth. Silks' Convenience was left untouched. From then on, the deaf outnumbered the hearing, and local organisers set up sign language classes alongside the bereavement counselling sessions in the meeting hall. None of the instructors knew the sign for Superb Lyrebird, so they used the one Tobey Silks had come up with. It happened that each person who had lost a loved one had a visitation from the bird. As if visited by a spirit, something alien and perfect, though it rarely did anything but scratch about, and sing, in a way that sent rainforests into the mind, holding back the smell of mud and crushed concrete with brilliant greens and cool clear water. Soon everyone visited by the vision had their own taxidermied lyrebird. Maree thought it a little unlikely herself. She couldn't say much about the loss of the town, since she had only been a little girl when the fourth landslide had happened, home ill from school, in safety. She barely remembered her brothers, let alone her classmates, and she had never had a vision of any bird. Still, she took the stuffed ones up on the anniversary of the landslips to the old armoury on the hill, and arranged them to watch over all, from early morning to sunset. If nothing happened, that, just that, was the miracle.

When the last of the lyrebirds had been set in elegant order on the wall, Maree signed to a window below, hoping her mother had got up and was pointing the telescope her way. The sign for vigil light. Up, across the valley, ran a ripple of gentle wind, that reached the silvering filamentaries of the birds and ruffled them a little, though not, as Maree remembered, holding her own hair, the way the real birds did, in the videos she had been shown.

HOW BEST TO BE BEST

Margot swam a length of the empty pool underwater, thinking of suffering. Above her, birds sang on repeat through the sound system. This was a new strategy. This was how to relax. At home, her white, aged cat was tugging roses from a dank vase by their stems and dropping them into the dark. The sun broke through the skylight above the pool and shone through the water onto Margot's back. Shade fell on Margot's house, turning the pale rag-rug on which Margot's aged cat had dropped herself a bluish colour. The cat also. More importantly, birds were singing and she couldn't identify them. She was twenty four and the word 'loathe' seemed the epitome of glamour. What matters is form – the extension of one arm over the tilted head, then the other. She swam. Margot was going to suffer and die one day. First she was going to pull herself through the water. Recently she had decided to stand within everything. Far advanced in this plan she had broken a boy's heart by politely turning him down. He had turned her friends against her, 'crazy Margot'. Margot vowed to live to a thousand, there in the pool. She broke the surface, she cut through the water like a finger through an envelope.

She traversed the water like a blunt object through the darkness of space. She did not understand physics very well. Somewhere not too far off a galaxy rotated, dragging broken glass and pink and blue vapours around it the exact way birdsong loops through a more sustaining atmosphere into a listening ear and out again, like a rose might spiral its petals around itself before it lets them drop. Margot's family loved her and they were all falling sick, one at a time, and going to the hospital and failing to walk out again, or managing it well enough, for a time.

She had fresh flowers in her locker beyond the pool; it was July and flowers pressed their froth everywhere upon her. She banished the flowers from her mind and thought of her body, the water. She touched the edge of the pool with outstretched fingers and turned. Above her invisible birds swam in their own elements, recorded in some wood in the south of England, or in cages, clutching invisible perches and puffing up their tiny throats before a microphone.

Margot was a nineteen-twenties flapper girl. She had far less elegance than her name urged. The hospital is the precise opposite of the swimming pool. She had peed a little in the pool, though she hadn't meant to, just on the shock of entry had let go. The water never let her go, nor any other body that passed through it: to live is to be involved with water that other people have touched and swallowed and pissed out. Something stung in the music and the bird song; an imperfection in the recording, or someone fiddling with it, and the noise went loud and fell off. Margot thought about the choice between the ladder at the far side of the pool and the ledge around it. Margot continued to swim and hear birdsong from under and above the surface of the water. There's something of an old book many times read about the idea of dying, as the ancient iceberg about the rain, and the rain about the blood pooling in an old woman's feet. There are flowers and vapours and bodies of water and bodies unknown, and that is fine, thought Margot.

Margot continued to swim. She did not, does not, have to leave.

MEANS

Brown birds were hopping and shrieking in the dusty golden grass. At least *that* was gold, thought Lina. At least that. And the sun, though it was turning oppressive. The young man had finished dousing himself at the pump. He lingered a while, standing so there was flattering light on his soaking body, and right where, if the girl would look up a little, she'd have to see him. But Lina was more than capable of feigning a blind spot, and eventually, he went off alone to lie down stiff and idle in the grass where the snakes were. Half-naked, thin and hairy, with his shirt bunched up for a pillow, with little sideways looks giving her the cow-eyes.

Lina breathed out and picked up her basket of washing. The sheets would get dusty, but that was what came with a drying wind. She took a glance over to where the man lay, dusty too and foolish. Her heart lurched. If someone could put that shirt on him, there would be more to the body, less shame in it. She might be young, and burning with all kinds of hungers, but she had thought things over plenty. Times were what they were, a dollar impossible, and it was no use getting tied in knots for lonely souls who looked on the verge of tantrum if they didn't get their way.

There were six cabins in the hamlet, most with a good-sized but near-barren square of land. Three families with heads of children coming in and out, one cabin hers, the other this stranger's, and one empty. One milk cow and three goats to speak of between the lot of them. Elsewhere in the landscape were the hills and the low, brown river. Years from now, after another war had blown through the world and she had taken a job as a typist in a small city, the woman would meet the man again by chance along a damp, rose-lined path through a park. That man and the one in the dust would be two quite different people, though they bore the same name and had just about the same face, if you squinted.

Long before then, it was an evening late in the summer and everything was dead from the heat. Lina was sweeping out the cabins. She did this in exchange for portions of cornmeal and coffee. Normally, she didn't sweep the lone man's cabin because he had so very little to pay her with, though he had taken the chance to ask her once, with a bright slyness, if there was anything he had she might want in exchange. No, she had said, she doubted that very much.

That evening he was gone to the nearest town with the three fathers of the camp. Lina was bored. She decided to get a sight of the sixth, empty cabin. For a book, she told herself. She knew there were still books in the cabin because the last man to live there had died in it and could not have taken them anywhere. She picked the door key from the window ledge and went in.

The cabin was irksomely dusty – everything was dusty, from coffee to bathwater – and for a while all Lina did was sweep. Why even complain? Lina was of the opinion that you could ignore the choke of dust in the air, but once you let it settle, once you let it in just to lounge over everything or on your person, it was like you were giving up on even trying to be civilised. It soothed her to shake off the lining of neglect that had grown over everything. When the house was clean she allowed herself appraisal of the bookshelf. The oddest books were there, many in red bindings with gold leaf on the pages. She hesitated to take one of these in case it might prove valuable, something to be accused of stealing. She decided on taking a battered, nicotine-colour specimen. A great cold thing that pulled her arms towards the ground when she held it. She couldn't say why take it at all. It seemed briefly charming, she supposed, something so heavy, so permanent in a world of whim and loss.

But while walking away from the cabin towards her own, a mood of uneasiness came on her. It was as if something lay on the ground alongside her feet in the deep dusky shadow. The thought pursued her. She willed herself not to be spooked, but at last submitted and looked down. There, to her left, was a long line of the bodies of men laid out head to feet; measuring yards of dead, hollowed-out corpses, there for an instant and then gone.

Lina raised her foot, but made no sound, feeling herself freeze up. It was her mind tricking her. No one else ought to come and help in a situation like this, she reasoned, because nothing was happening, and later there'd be talk, so you should just keep on and do not scream. Replace the book, she told herself, but she couldn't replace the book, because what if, when she turned again, that line of bodies once more stretched out, one after another, parched and staring upwards? A wind was gusting, making sounds her ears understood as a rising and eternal bell of distress. The closest house was the lone man's place, though no lights were on. Nothing was happening. She kept walking at the same steady speed until she reached it, slipped the book on his step and headed quickly for home, wiping her hands on her apron. The darkness was wide, and that night as long, though it was all her imagination, she thought.

Towards dawn one of the goats cried out in the uncanny voice of a child, waking Lina. She lay the rest of the hour in bed scanning the boards of the ceiling, imagining herself a dead woman, hollowed out by desiccation, until she shook the notion off, and rose to get the hotcakes started.

When she came out to fetch water, the book was gone from where she'd left it.

And that was that, apart from once, in the depths of the next night, when she woke to a clinging, moist air draped over her face and the sound from outside of…something. Like a chair squealing over a wooden floor. Then a flash, not of light, that rushed in under the door and through the room like the wind, like wind's shadow, without disturbing anything.

The young man was never the same afterwards. Something in his life had changed. He had grown unexpectedly rich, or at least, had prospects of wealth. There was a bustle of activity around his cabin. Porters coming and going, loading up his possessions, slowly removing him from their dry little scuff on the earth. Lina noted how his eyes had lost their sense of need, yet how steady his gaze had become, how still and how upright his bearing, though at that time he was still dreadfully thin.

At last he stood out smiling on his porch step telling the hamlet his intent to leave, and distributing gifts – tobacco, tea, pencils for the children, a bag of cinder toffee for her sweet tooth. Then he packed up his belongings, rode out waving. The dust driven up behind his horse was the usual type, but it seemed to swirl in suggestive ways, and hung a while behind like tall, sparse figures, watching him go.

So when it came to Lina meeting him all those years later she expected to find him to be ruined, to have that hounded look of a man who makes wild bargains and is handed his years of regret. Instead he was just as calm, as he walked beside her through the green park, and talked endlessly, and was still rich, even more so. More so, and time and a richer diet had filled him out, put a lustre on his skin. She began to think that the incident with the book had been something she had embellished. She had after all been very lonely in those days, without means beyond her own capability. And she had been capable most days, it was just that sometimes the mind gets stretched out and suffers, and the world seems wilder and more dangerous than it could possibly be.

They stood a while between two rose beds, one side all yellow, the other red, and he pointed to a flower from the red side, a great fat red dew-sprinkled thing much like all the others on the bush. He held it up, still attached by the stem, guided her by the chin until her face poked right into the bloom. Lina, seeing no reason not to, inhaled deeply. She smelled nothing awry in the folded heart of it. The man she had known, after all, had always behaved in that sort of a way, if not so masterfully.

After they were married they moved into a large, pristine townhouse that flanked the same park. From every position in the living room, library or even the bathroom there was no way to avoid that expensive view of the pillars of oaks, and beneath these rolling a lush stretch of grass, and flowerbeds cutting into it, swollen to overflowing with white stocks and burst red poppy heads.

One night, Lina told him the story of the book, the corpses laid out like beached fish looking up at the stars, only for an instant, mind, and the moans on the wind, the strange flash that had blown through her cabin. She told it after dinner by the fire first as remembrance of the dust-choked old times and then at the meat of the story as if a joke, because that was the best way.

He slapped his knee at the end, laughing. Lina continued on to some other story. She was the sort who could make anything amusing, if it was necessary. He poured out wine for them both. A cold sweet wine Lina couldn't get the taste for but would drink anyway, because it was there to be had and was once considered rare. She thought no more might come of the foolishness with the book, what her eyes had or hadn't seen. Thinking to herself instead about her moments of resistance; of snakes and golden grass shushing back and forth over a young body lying amongst it, and the snap of dust-streaked washing on the line. Then she ran out of story. After a silence, at last, and in just about a whisper he leaned forward in his chair and said, "All that story just now would have been the thing for the boy to hear."

"Maybe then you could tell it to him, to his face," Lina said, in a steady voice, "when you next get the chance."

The man laughed again. "Not for a while, not for a while," he said, raising his full glass up to his teeth and holding it there a while, before he drank it all down. Then he pulled her close, leaning in for a kiss. Lina tilted her face to receive it, and stared out at the space beyond her life. Through the window the park stood verdant and muted in the failing light, utterly devoid of birds, or snakes, or dust of any kind.

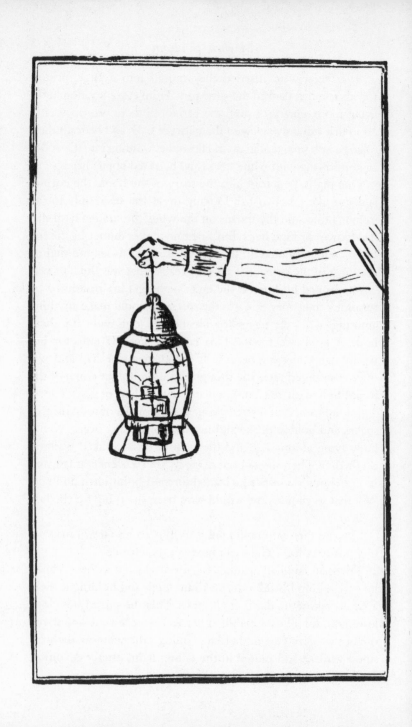

THE PURVEY

The heavy brass lantern stood on the white corner table of the conservatory, noticed by no one but us, and that was unacknowledged. The two of us crammed into the wicker loveseat, watched bees from the apiary scrambling in the mint outside. Mourners making turns in the teak-panelled main room held the deceased's dark wine glasses as props of gesture. The air in here vegetal, perfumed with rankness, spots of mould on the rim of the windows, the drone outside, the drone within. I murmured, "Isn't it close?"

But you just stared, smiling fixedly, at a small girl reaching up to cut herself a wedge of quiche.

"She wouldn't like me to have come," you said, still smiling.

I reached for your hand.

"Don't," you said. I pulled back, stung.

An image of the dead woman came to mind; the seconds before I'd killed her. She was laughing – she would always laugh at the worst times, and smile too, you had that in common. Sitting in the other wicker chair she was, laughing, fizzing a cigarette from her lips.

"You'll never get him," she'd said to you. "He won't have such a mouse."

"But I don't want him," you'd said. "I only want to show that you're nothing to him. To anyone."

The thickets of mourners turning about greeted each other with tilted heads. The little girl bit into her quiche. Crumbs scattered with a noise I could hear across the room. I rose and went to the lantern.

"What are you doing now?" you whispered. I opened the drawer and took out a beeswax candle.

"Monster," you said, as I lit it and placed it in the lantern. It had looked like a theatre piece before. Now gleaming, full, it was almost right.

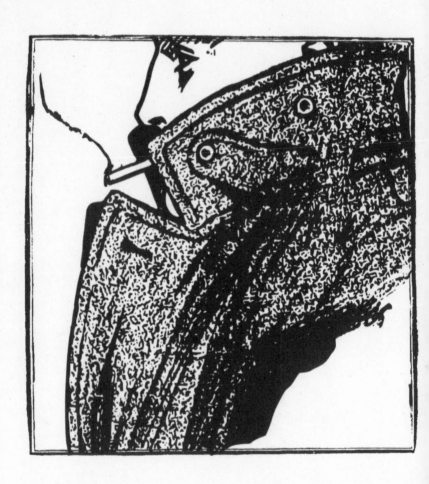

FOLK NOIR

A man is walking along the edge of the grey fens, whistling. There's a crack and a cry, and the sound of long grass blown by a sudden wind from the sea.

The detective smokes a cigarette standing in a pool of light. A car draws up. He throws his suitcase in the back seat. Beside the car a field full of yellow stands grey under the full moon. The moon is always full on nights like these. There's something unsavoury about crops at night, the winking drama of poppies caught in headlights as the car passes.

There's a woman who knows. She has darting eyes and a blood-black mouth. She's the baker, her oven backs onto the butcher's rooms. God of the idle and those who help themselves. On the stone was a kind of message. Words are hard to come by. Spies smile with fresh eggs held out in one hand, a pistol in the other. It's a known fact a ring of mushrooms will sprout over a corpse put too shallow in the ground.

Darkness drags itself down the country lanes like a wounded man. The detective smokes in his room above the inn. Looks between two pieces of paper with handwriting on it: the will, the lover's note. A notebook open on the table; sketches of the stone ring jut like bad teeth. There was code here. It said always close the gate behind you. It said don't trust anyone but yourself. Sound of a scuffle outside. Right on cue the detective pulls back the curtain. Nothing at all lay out there in a pool of blood. No body, slumped in a pool of country darkness. If he'd been quicker, maybe. If he could understand these people. Both detective and villagers talk with their back molars, but mutual comprehension is fancy talk, both ways. Euphemism rides under every tongue.

All's very carefully, cutely hidden away. Take a drink. It ain't tea in that cup. Wash that round your boots. Slip into something more rumour, more horse-brass hung above the snarling fire. No one here'll leave a kiss on your fern-ticked gravestone. Ask anyone in lipstick, anyone caught dancing in the fields. That's tomorrow, son. A small town's a cage like any other. The detective trudges back to his room. Tomorrow is for the suspects. He suspects his own death.

And into the four poster bed he curls up with his boots on, wrapped in song from the women singing hymns as they knit in a room upstairs, and the sound goes down slow like a loss through the body. Thinking of it this way: stone is always a grave. Mud in the fen, black feinting mass of woodlands, bunting hung in the dark of a butcher's window. And nothing in this place flickers like a match struck. Snuffing the flame, the insects come. The jarring beat of them, *set-set*, going all damn night.

STICK TO ME, PEEL FROM ME

After *Stoker*

Pleasure is a shade falling over your face barring the eyes, which glow with feelings that frighten and persuade. I have arranged my shoes in their boxes from the smallest size to the largest, around my body, which is only one size, the size it has been since I was thirteen. I am an adult now but a coiled one, waiting in this body yet to spring. And it is summer time, and the moss is hanging from the trees, and all your letters come floating down the stairs to make themselves creased in my hands.

I go hunting in the woods for a shade that looks like you, like a deer or bird of you, on slender legs like my own. I get the butt of the gun against my shoulder: I like the shock of muscle and bone as it throws back at triggering. I love the muted sounds nature puts on, but sounds made by me, the shock of me, the best. I am afraid of my fingers on the pulsing wound in the deer's throat, on the bird's hanging neck. I am made to think of prey by your voice in a letter. I watch you cross the schoolyard many years later many hours later the same day in silken and flat light, like my blouse, like one of my pleated skirts stuck to the thighs has inflected everything. I see a playpark with my name on it, my name in my fingers on the keys of the family piano, afraid at the sound of them, deep, as your fingers ride along towards mine, and the sound throws me back.

If I name you I name myself and you, or something with the shape of you, takes a name from out the bottomless satin hat and with a faint flourish says it's all for me, this performance, this sleight of hand, this obfuscation of shadow and wild, wanting eyes that seem to hold all that I will one day know, and I recoil. A gun or a garrotte is neither a high tree branch nor a pair of heels nor a walk through sultry night with a beloved, but with me, with you, it is all those things.

Come with me, come with me, into the cellar where the lightbulb sputters, swings, knowing it merely repeats the old rhythms, knowing it will be outside of the house where I am cracked into another form like a baton against a magic hat and the dead rabbit becomes a live one, thumping. Come with me or don't, so the house sprites follow me out, like you did follow me, sit too close, at the keys, air too close, a hum of music, like myself alone without you, this pleasure, in the dark, to a liaison, to a treason to saying my name in your voice. I hold my throat and feel its pulse. I blink through visions of a cracked neck, dirt streaming over me and blood also. Viscous or cracked dry it washes away like nothing but the night remains behind and all we've done. Even saying this word blood is trespass. I am slight. I am obscene in a poet's dress imagined by Hollywood. You've seen me now I am disappearing over the spattered fields, and through the music, let me be pleased, let my ways be snipped shut, for only I, above all, spattered too, pulse metronomic, can hear her changing now.

PHARMAKÓS

Pharmakós (Greek: φαρμακός*): the ritualistic sacrifice or exile of a human scapegoat to appeal to the benevolence of a god.*

Our pharmakós woman sits bound loosely to a rock on a hillside, licking the foil of her yoghurt lid. They'd left her that, anyway. She can see the stars fine. She can see the bodies up there, born of the hours of looking that we have lost how to do.

She hears the city begin to murmur into panic. A city a mile or two away. She hears as all the people in the crisp dusk coalesce into a collective realisation: not far beyond the city there is a bulging of the lid of the sea, a high wave with darker shadows of seaweed like tentacles wriggling in the building waves. Not that the form of THE END truly matters at all – it is the seconds before it that do. She is feeling mostly in this moment a fizzy mix of defiant and defeated. A tear slides down her cheek and into her mouth, tear as soft dissolve, tear as *make me*. Then the sour sweet taste of yoghurt makes her think of her Greek grandmother, who hated the stuff, but made it for her husband because it was the one thing he could love her for.

There are seas where the dead lie so thick they are pressed into a layer of silt the colour of yoghurt that sits at the bottom, under all that water, waiting to be churned up briefly by the fall of the next shipwrecked boat. She presses a hand to her mouth and lets the plastic pot of her last meal go. Eventually her tears dry up, her sobs fall back and the quiet settles, and the water, as it will, is rising to quiet everybody, or just her, depending. From her rock on the hill the Pharmakós woman makes that deal like you do with all the dead already broken up to beach dust, she makes her deal with the starry void and the wall of water; it comes, it comes, it sweeps her body back.

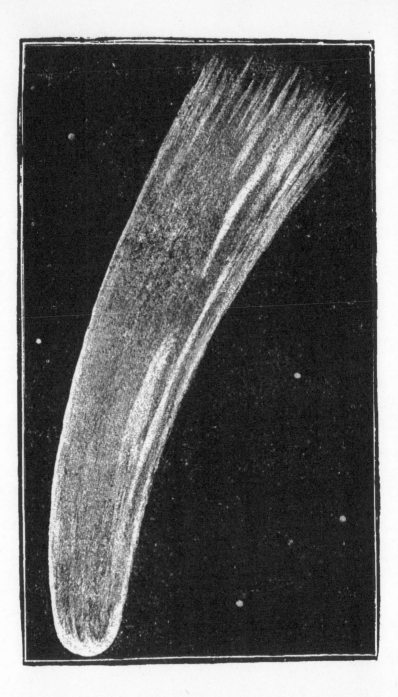

MARY SOMERVILLE'S CELESTIAL DISRUPTION

This did not happen –

In a navy blue frock, one of the most influential female scientists of the Georgian and Victorian eras stands at the end of her garden in Burntisland staring directly at the sun, being only seven or eight years old at this time, and unaware of the sun's affect upon optics, never mind the mathematics that swings these grand systems all about together without ever touching, so long as you don't look.

Life is vivid: through a gap in a stone wall the firth in placid form is teeming with possibility, tidal salts, tiny anemones and slippery bladderwrack. Industry about her is carrying on, on the backs of the poor. This she will know, and feel in response pity, a distinctly lesser feeling than comfort, and the pleasures laid platterwise by good breeding. For the poor only talk in a brutal language. And in other countries under the genteel crooked thumb of the empire they talk fighting talk, fighting-to-stay-alive talk, angered at the British, which is, to the British, unfathomable and unforgiveable.

In free countries they speak in French and Italian, and Mary Somerville will find it *juste*. But for now she is a rather little and uneducated *girrul* in Coarse Northern Lands, speaking the language of the possessed, dizzy with her pencil, shy, rebellious against her station. This is how we like her best.

Rather than the sun she is in point of fact now staring at a comet, so henceforth a comet is coming, and she has seen it, and is measuring its progress by the seaward wall. The angles are a mystery to her, but the sense of imminent cataclysm is easily graspable. 'Cataclysm' neither in the medieval sense nor in the modern sense: the Georgian sense of destruction – neatly formed and highly reasonable to the senses.

Dear little Mary, come in now, away. The comet is shining like a compass on an old map, brilliant points of a star, with two tails carving silver above the southern horizon. Very dull poems are being composed on it, as you look on it, trembling, following its brilliance in the dark brilliance of your mind.

There it is, against the thin layer of atmosphere it has just pierced. There it is, a silent fiery shriek, nearing and now nearing the Earth. And Mary Somerville, her whole life planned out in dinner parties, covert learning, scientific scrutiny, grief, loss of fortune, Italian seasons, obsequiousy and bloody-mindedness, at seven or eight years old when we see her here, witnesses the comet smash itself apart mid-air, boiled vapour and rock spraying down, deviant, hungry and impatient for its own obliteration with the larger body of the planet.

A shockwave ripples across the surface of the sky.

Come away, Mary Somerville, you've so much to do, and to not quite understand. Shrapnel pieces fling in all directions in meteorite ceilidh. Only a little girl in her navy dress at the end of her garden watches it happen. For it is only for her, observant, refusing not to not look. Rocks on fire and splittered with nickel-iron ore fall down upon her. Sizzling through her skirt ends, pummelling her forehead. Mary Somerville future Queen of Science is knocked to the ground, and lies there, on the grass, staring at the heavens now.

Does she die?
This did not happen.
But – even so – is she hurt?

A COVEN OF TWO

After *Practical Magic*

It's always been something carried in our blood, the story goes. My sister comes to me in my sleep, and I in hers. My red-headed sister, the one dancing lightly over the earth, wrinkling her nose, free of the choices I have made, while I lie burdened with a double dose of hers and my own.

It's a thick stew that feeds nothing.

She, acrid-yellowing, burns a hole in me with her absence, visible only in the dark, when we sleep thousands of miles apart. I like that I am purity and she is slut, and that we are the same person, bound palm to palm. Our great-great grandmother built a house on the bones of her lovers, after escaping a hanging by means of her craft. Of my dead husband, we no longer speak. My sister comes to me in my sleep and in hers and pulls me up from the grey syrup of being alone. I make the mistake of writing it down.

My daughters walk to school like blips in time. I teach them a clove paste is all it takes to numb the body from all taunts. A face that permits no one to take anything from it. I wish, I bless. Decay runs out over the fields.

I am trying to peel myself out of the history of our femaleness, constructing a miserable, invisible self, until my sister comes to me while we both sleep and takes me to the window. The moon has a halo around it, which means a curse.

Isn't it too indulgent to be sisters, to be cursed. Well, it just so happens. Indulgence is in our blood, and entwined in blood, our skeletons. Milk-blooded weavers and hungry.

We kill a man twice, we kill a man bloodless and stamp wallowing on his shallow grave with blessed muddy feet. Plant lavender for luck, roses plant themselves. We drink cursed cocktails piss-coloured clumsy things, at midnight. We close a circle. We whisper through chapped lips. We fail. A man comes, holding my letter, but I pull out his one blue eye and one green. We mind narrative drive as a thing for pistons and not for us. We repeat through our pacing, our fancy interiors.

My sister falls asleep on my bed. From a vein in her arm to a painted veil over mine, this sleep, this longing stitched up. We close a circle and spit, drive the talkative ash of men clear and far away from our rose-ringed door.

THE LANGUAGE
OF HEAVEN

I want to tell you about this other film I saw, one night when you were out sticking twigs in your hair and shoving your hand into the mouths of foxes, you dank, fleshy monster. This film was about a woman who had lost her snakes.

She had owned a serpentarium, at least, that's what it was called in the film. It was a snake house – there were frogs also – that was perched in the edge of a village on an island where the rain lived. This woman had angered the local community by keeping snakes and charging their children money to see and touch them. She charged tourists too, but no one cared about them.

So one night, a father opened up all the vivariums, even for the poisonous snakes. None of the snakes were awake, but the music made you think something violent was going to happen. I suppose the violence was in the man, not the snakes. In fact, I'm sure of it.

The rest of the film shows the woman adjusting to her new role as snakeless bystander. There's a love interest, and a showdown. Some of the snakes are caught, but one bites the father – here's the violence of before finally coming home – and he dies in a field of cows.

Then it got weird. The winter came and the snakes died. And the locals were troubled by their ghosts, and they had the woman perform a cleansing rite. They wouldn't ask a priest to do it, because on that island the Catholics are generally disliked.

In a desolate anger, she raises the snakes from the dead, and has their half-rotted snake-corpses enter the homes of the locals –

Anyway, not to spoil it, but I'm glad I watched this film without you. I'm rich with ideas, drenched in them, like a misty, flooded island in a sluicing sea, like a boa swimming away through a cut in a cold bog. And I think there is no room for you on either side of the film or my telling of it.

GALLERY PIECE

The wood splits here. On one side of the fire break the trees are white birches, but on the other they are so densely black where they stand in the rock shadow that we cannot tell what sort of tree they are. It is to be supposed pine, given the altitude.

In the centre, the murderess. There is the yellow fog of sulphur, from the hot spring that bubbles out from a rock and flows luxuriously towards the town in the valley. The murderess, having climbed here from below, has chosen to wash her heavy garments in the hot spring to get the blood out, and in leisure watch it dally between the silky river grasses and tiny warm-water fish. To this end she has removed her outer clothes and begun beating them on a yellow-stained rock. She grunts from effort, she watches her hands and forearms redden, the blood sets in place.

In a wide concentric circle around her are the woods. A circle above her, the summit of the mountain. At some point, she has done all she can. She has washed her face and thinks, it appears, of the angels. Floating child heads with pigeon wings stirring up the marshy air. A circle that confounds and comforts her. Torches from below dance through the white part of the forest. Below and rising. Yellow fire. Dogs like smudges. There is the scrabble of black earth, there is the steaming river. The angels have advised the murderess of the forthcoming mob, and she has chosen for herself the river. She steps full in, enveloped, and folds her arms. Something in the shadow at the edge of the frame has taken up her hand.

RITUAL STITCHES,
GOOD RED WOUNDS

Muggy air. Plum in up to the wrists. Picking rinds from the stopped waste disposal. He's pulled the machinery out so nothing can get you. But you know there are so many ways in which you can be gnawed upon. It scares you into effrontery, into brittle spectacle. No roses, you say, no damn chocolates, like thin poise is going to help you live intact.

Below your knees, he calls out your name in a disgusted tone, and when you do not answer him right away, when you whip your hand out of position and just stand, inching, he swears and hauls himself out brandishing a tiny wrench. He, too, stands a moment, considering. He is a quiet man, generally, but prone to staring, fits of high, echoing laughter. He picks up the nearest glass, yours, and throws it very precisely, an inch away from your head. It smashes on the white washed wall and falls in neat bits to the floor, and he makes you sweep it up by simply swivelling his eyes to it every time he is in the kitchen. He drags your hand towards the sink, to where the machine has started up again. He only pulls away at the last second, feigning a joke.

You will curse him, but not at this moment, the two of you shuddering at one another in the sunset-lit kitchen with the small white cat mewling at its empty water dish.

No, it will be years later, when you are living in a clapperboard house, or else in the cabin, or else in a high flat looking out on a dirge of a city where the greasy sky always threatens rain too weak to wash anything clean. When you have run from him, lost the cat but finally made it away, and have the energy to put to use a certain set of skills you have developed.

You have made sure the sea is never very far away, never more than an hour on foot and by train. You take the last thing you have of his, which you kept through your loathing. It's an expensive pen, a hip flask, a china saucer that belonged to his dear old mum.

The sea, or the ocean, is perfectly calm, like glass, like you. When you throw this item in, the perfectly calm sea begins to boil. There are birds in a great flock, coming closer, wheeling over you and the spot in the sea that is boiling. This is a very simple spell. If it does not work, and you merely throw the thing in and the sea accepts it with its usual indifference, you will feel petty and uncomfortable, and go home to your high flat, your cabin, your clapperboard house and stew a while. But in this instance it works. And the sea is boiling and a dark stain spreads briefly across it, and the birds start screaming and nipping in at your loose hair.

And then the sea dies down, and the moment is over. And you go home, and you make a complex casserole and pour yourself red wine from your cellar, from your cupboard, from a box, and drink it down with relish. You'll read of the effects in a strange story your sister will forward to you. The light from the page will illuminate your face. There will be no crowing, no surge of power. No one will ever connect you to this, nor mention you by name in any article concerning him. But there will be words you linger on. *Academic. Malfunction. Pooled. Drainage ditch.* After this there will always be a light on somewhere, flickering against your skin. The colour of a white internet page, the swarming blush of the sunsets when you had no way of knowing what you do now, of your brutal, anonymous capacity.

NOSTALGIA TREMENS

She was excited for the way the sweet would taste in his mouth. She cut away the parchment paper, sprinkled salt, then rolled the pizza cutter back and forth across the surface, frowning. Kiss-sized pieces, she thought as she twisted wrappers around each cube. She slipped a couple in the pocket of her skirts.

When that was done she wiped a damp cloth down her neck, pushing against the texture of it, and went to wring it out over the porch. Over the dog bowl because she was in that careless a mood. There was a sunshower over her neighbour's garden where her dog, a heavy boned mutt, was sleeping in the prim grass.

"Yah," she called to Cuddy, but he didn't twitch. Strange for him to be over there, she thought. For the first few months the neighbours would take Cuddy in and feed him all kinds of food that upset his stomach. So she'd trained him out of wandering, at least in that direction.

She walked down the steps and along the path and out the gate and up the neighbour's path brushing by the lavender bush and across their grass towards Cuddy. A sprinkler was going intermittently, with the dog right under it, coloured darker by the water.

She put her arms around Cuddy's neck.

"Cuddy" she said, and the creature raised its head. It wasn't her dog. His or her darker grey all his own. Great wide grey jaw, drooling gums hanging like spoiled meat, and pinprick eyes like a patch of the interstellar medium compressed in its head by

89

two strong thumbs. She didn't let her arms drop, not right away.
The dog started making a noise like when her neighbour sat on
his motorbike and kicked.

"Hey," she said, and slowly moved her hand so it was resting
lightly on the dog's huge shoulder. "There, now." She could
feel the space around her contracting. The dog breathed harder,
and suddenly she could smell cotton candy and leather. Cotton
candy and beer, the very particular brand of beer she used to
drink on porches, through stormy nights, in a particular east
coast town, back when she was eighteen and finding out
America for the first time.

She started to laugh. Candyfloss. Hints of cigarette, funnel
cake – or was it waffles, from the diner? The dog showed her
the interlock of its front teeth. Drool was coming in at her
own mouth. She laughed and then stopped. She felt a great
kinship with the dog: it was sodden, ugly and smelled like a
night out on the boardwalk with the wrong crowd. She pulled
out a caramel and unwrapped it. The dog began to bark in her
face. She did not flinch. The barking rose in pitch. She pulled
out a second caramel for the dog.

Before she could unwrap the treat, the sprinkler stuttered
on. Her dress grew damp patches dark grey like the dog. It was
going to bite her throat out. In her fist would be the caramel
that would be later found in neat abundance on the kitchen
counter. By the paramedics she supposed, by the police, by
him. The dog snapped, flecking her face. She pushed her neck
forward, smiling. Yes, the dark gummy maw smelled exactly like
a day at the seaside. Well and isn't that enough for a fine Friday
afternoon?

The dog lunged and bit down. There was a pause while her
brain tabulated the signals. Yellow teeth embedding in her. A
crushing sense. Foam. The dog held her in its jaws and jerked
backwards and forwards. Growls vibrated and her blood started
screaming in her ears. She did not resist, but to her shame did
seize a little into red fire, her body all at once deciding, against

her wishes, to shake itself and pound feet and fists against the lawn. Brown dribbles of caramel oozed between her own teeth.

Lastly she could just taste sweet, and feel the world at tilt. And then there was something coming for her, a blur across the garden. Salted caramel is no great substitute, she thought, for good sea air.

THE ROMANTIC COMEDY

You want the wrong things. The camera glories in the horse at full gallop through russet woods. And on its back you the bride in white, urging onwards. Hoof beat, snapped twig, threshing sounds of the undergrowth. Music swells and the branches of the trees catch at your veil, and you are every heroine of romance, ripping loose her stitches to get out of the picture. Into the open field. No more compulsive acquiescence. No more smiling on cue. No more men standing too close explaining how to exist, believing, if left to your own devices, you'd not quite manage such a feat. You want the wrong things. You resist, you run.

This is the town behind you: the town of old stone or skyscrapers and crisp smoke. The town of the snarky, ugly man who is most desirable. The town of the handsome man who speaks with his eyes and slow smile and pristine bulk of his masculinity. The town of kiss, pull back, laugh, kiss with the right man and no one else. The town of it's just your fault for never knowing what you want. The town of what's new with women this decade. The town of unacknowledged debasement. The town of fake snow and empty streets circling around each other forever. The town without any kind of scent. The town of one carefully messed up desk to show you are a busy heterosexual woman. God, it's a big town. A capital city, though it tries not to let on. You drive the horse onwards and the sun is lowering in the sky. Red and autumn spill everywhere, and the hills besides.

For your whole life there had been just enough irony to let you breathe – but an oxygen mask is not a good alternative to the air being real. The music says to you, keep flitting. The music says to you, this is narrative, and soon the close, and soon the laughter and a hard, ending kiss. Turf kicks up behind you. A dull thump against the twisting strain. Because you want too much, and that's the trouble with you women. You want the wrong things. Like flesh and life, like a wet heart and nimble, unheld fingers. The only choice is to protect yourself with the things you've been given. The horse rears and dashes and you are alone. In a painting of a beautiful woman turned away in a landscape. You don't want to be alone, do you? A giant sign saying, hollow cry. *Is there any way to get free of the mind?* Only as a punchline, only as a kiss.

Waiting in the town, there's the man thumbing red roses in the long golden wheat. Smile coming slowly unhinged from his face. There's the ex-loverboy miming the acceptable level of anger and despair and acceptance and there's his new love beside him, his consolation prize. There's the best friend, smiling and waving, having no thought in her head other than you, but this is straight, of course it's a straight way of thinking. No lips touching other lips that can be soft red and hot – and maybe you don't want love at all, maybe you want other wrong things. The pastoral strapped to your chest. The season turning and tender brittling, and for a second, a drawing down through a channel of wind and leaves. A fractured wholeness like an exploded dandelion, no strings attached. And here's the road where you thought you would leave. Fields and scenic birds rising over it. Music rising over it. Are you leaving? Do you really want to go? And you are loved by something creeping a long blue shadow behind, and you're running? You, running. You start to open your mouth, and in the wide open empty field, in the wide valley of all these stringencies, you gently call out – lips bluish now – the last and stale and only thing you cherish – your own name.

A SILENT
DOCUMENTARY
THROUGH A
TERRIBLE PLACE

The camera pans across the high hedge until it reaches a low opening; a set of stairs leading upwards. Smoothly we progress, drawn by the line, by the fireworks of neon lichen on the rough thick bare walls, upwards. A narrow passage, a stone weight.

At the top of the stairs, a tapestried curtain passes over a doorway, and this is drawn back, and we must enter, and the room is revealed in breadcrumb pieces: this carved chair. That altar. The figures seated around us, facing forward, skin gleaming or sagged, a snatch of plain fabric, rich, eyelashes flittering. They face the altar, yes. It is only that when we name it. On the altar, a glass bottle full of soft shapes suspended in what looks viscous. We do not need to know what they are, materially. Up beyond the altar is another curtained opening, another spine-straight set of stairs, a room beyond, and on we move. Come, keep going.

In this room there are dark pews arranged as in the first, white paint flaking in the grey recesses of the walls, and statues, faces broken, hands outreached to bless the long-gone breakers of their faces. On each pew, a line of shoes, leather battered, stitching crude. We follow a central passage of the eye of this camera towards – towards what comes out of the darkness. A gutter on the floor brims with ambivalent fluids. But the next entrance leads to a corridor angled steeply up, lined with hanging baskets. The kind of waypath found in a hospital, though the walls are plain, no tidemark of colour here, no arrow-lines on the floor pointing out the way to the ward we need.

The flowers in the baskets are white and profuse, and you could imagine the smell. You don't though. Now there is someone ahead of us, and she is extremely tall, and it is best that we cannot see her face. She walks small-footedly, her hair is bound back in a white wimple. Her right hand drags against the wall at an unsettling angle that presses wall against knuckles and fingernails alike. The camera permits us, guides us, to look at the marks she leaves there. Soon there has to be an opening; a heavy oak door with great black iron hinges. You hope for a garden.

Yes, there is the door, you were right. There is order to this universe, there is a creed implicit in the unbroken cut from beginning to perceptible end. The promise of fair passage, of visual justice. This is a life, you start to think, perhaps a life lived through the history of a pre-modern century. Or all of human history, telling some greater story you need time to understand, when you will arrange your thoughts into place and secure yourself. But this is the medieval moment unspooling, in stone, fabric, candle, fevered, harsh and full of miracles.

The door opens silently outwards, there has never been any sound. A white space ahead. Then words, in characters and a language you cannot read, rise to emblazon in bold type on a grey wheat field in full sway.

I WAS AT LAST A ROMANTIC COMEDY ABOUT CORRUPTION AND DECAY

It wasn't anything special. It was the kind of film you go to see when you're pulling a sick day and your pal suggests it, just to get you out of the house. We accidentally bought tickets to the fancy screening, the one entered through glass doors to a lounge ringed with black and white photos of celebrities who had never been there, but who might, possibly, stop in for complimentary soft drinks and tiny popcorn in old fashioned bags. The lounge was empty except for the wry staff, noting how obviously we did not belong. Screen 13. We sat right in the middle, on comfortable seats that came with their own little tables. The thirteenth screen reserved for the lucky few. Or just us, at 2pm on a sunny Wednesday.

The film was one neither of us had heard of, and was listed in the pamphlet as a romantic comedy about corruption and decay. I thought it would be Swedish, and wasn't sure. My friend thought it would be something like *Happiness* or *Storytelling*. I told her I hadn't seen either, and she was about to let me know more of their qualities, when the ads stopped and the trailers began.

"You get the first one," I said.

So she was a psychological thriller about suave, traitorous spies, and then I was an adventure film about the arctic attacking people, she was a drama about a magic mentally ill person and I was at last a romantic comedy about corruption and decay.

"They can't show the trailer for the film we're about to watch," my friend said, crossing her arms. I threw popcorn in my mouth until I didn't have to say anything.

The title came up, followed by a landscape of American trees in the autumn, seen from above. I settled further into my chair.

"This is good," she said. I nodded.

First we met Gina, a girl from the suburbs who liked to lie in the dirt of her back garden, where everything had died. Then we met her family. Her mother in the kitchen, her dad watching the TV, her brother who was dead and lived in photographs. Gina's job was to be the film's idea of an American woman. Then she met Peter. They went up into the hills together. It time for Gina to get mad at Peter, or the other way around. So they did.

"I think there's going to be an apocalypse," I said.

And there was. The rain fell in black lines on the ridge. The land started to slip away. Peter and Gina clutched at each other. Then they fell a long way. Gina walked with a limp until she forgot. They walked for miles through a narrow ravine that was covered in white flowers. They forgave each other. We started throwing popcorn at the screen.

Gina's family appeared at the mouth of the ravine. The road to town was right behind them. But it was clear something was wrong. They were a hallucination. Gina was dead. Peter was looking for her. Or it was the other way around. A great bell began to chime, so loud it seemed to be coming from the empty space above out heads, invisibly rending it apart. I covered my ears. The soundtrack would likely get an Oscar nod, but I didn't think it would win. Gina walked out of the ravine, down through the din and on into the suburbs, walking till her limp returned. She saw her house. She went to look in the window. There was Peter. There *she* was, in Peter's arms. She screamed as the pair slowly turned to her, and smiled.

"The cinematography is really excellent," I whispered.

"Perfect," my friend said, shuffling in her fizzy drink with her straw.

The other Gina opened her mouth and made a clicking sort of groan by compressing her vocal cords. Original Gina backed away. Suddenly a hole opened up in the road. Nothing but a warbling blankness, like a glitch in a video game. Her foot clipped through, and she tripped. She picked herself up and looked at her undamaged hands. The camera faced her head on, unmoved by her confusion and grief.

"Breaking the fourth wall? Yeah, how novel," I said.

"Where am I?" Gina asked.

"You're in the cinema," my friend shouted.

"I'm watching a movie," said Gina. "A really boring one about two women sitting in the dark being clever."

Suddenly Original Peter was slumped next to her. He looked like he was dying. He was free.

"I love you," they said, one after the other.

"I love the news," my friend said. "I love documentaries. And thrillers about gay geniuses."

I dabbed my eyes with a handkerchief. Peter had died at last and his ghost had crawled out of his corpse to love Gina in an even more perfect way, without touching. Gina moved to a lakehouse provided by witness protection. She was trying to make a new life for herself as a book editor who never goes to work. One day a hole opened up in the ice in the lake. Gina stared into it.

"I love you," she said to the hole in the lake. The hole froze over again, and there was a long shot of Gina, bawling, mouth smoking, couchant on a perfectly white field. For a while she had a habit of buying small gifts for herself, wrapping them up in pink crepe and carefully opening them, pretending they were from someone else.

"Boo!" I yelled.

"Pinterest," my friend muttered. The last gift was the keys to the kingdom of heaven, which apparently locked with a Yale.

"Why would you be so indulgent with yourself?" she asked.

I shook my head. I was trying to work out the cryptic messages on the walls of the lakehouse. I thought advertising had really tried to get sneaky on us.

"You're going to have to end happily soon," I said at the screen, as Gina was baking a pie for her housewarming.

"That fruit doesn't grow at that time of the year," my friend said. "Those are probably wads of painted gum."

"But she looks so happy."

"I guess that's the most important thing," my friend said flatly.

Gina sat at a typewriter, writing a new ending for herself.

"Very good, love," my friend yelled, adding something crass I won't repeat here. Gina rolled her eyes. I liked that we were in this together. I only wanted maybe to get a better look at the furnishings in her new house, which a whole team had put together and then lit so well. Gina danced to a happy song. Gina ran herself a bubble bath. The rest of the film was more Romantic twists, tripping and falling into various human voids and loving them in agonised ways. Eventually the lake unfroze and lapped with rotting fish, each with a ring in its mouth, all meant for Gina's beautiful hand. Put there perhaps by the ghost. That was up for debate; the meaning was deeply ambiguous, given the rings melted as she touched them, and were absorbed into the soil at the banks of the lake. So it was wish fulfilment in the end, if you try really hard. It personally aligns with my view of the world. I can't recommend it for everyone, but for a way to kill time: yes, by all means.

A CHARM FOR THE
WORLD AS IT IS

A charm for autumn light, and your skirts sopping at the water's edge. A charm for raising your blood, so that you can walk, trailing dirt and leaves, away from the water and through the park. A charm for knowing history. A charm for silencing doubt. A charm for doubt. A charm for making a lie apparent. A charm for silencing the dull ache that returns to you as you remember everything the world is and still is and continues to be. A charm for your awful pain at it. A charm for your body's flesh that persists in being your flesh. A charm against the din of the nearing road. A charm for the people walking out of the fog and into your circle of damp misery. A charm against politically-induced depression. A charm against Brexit. A charm for compassion. A charm for all who drown. A charm for all who drown in the Mediterranean. A charm for those who do not drown. A charm for them. A charm against despair. A charm for autumn light. A charm for the buses, and the people on the buses, all normal and good folk, arms in slings, legs kicking against buggies, eyes blinking behind specs, heads bent over phones. A charm for them. A charm for the people you walk by, who are staring, of course they are staring, but doubt themselves for doing it and turning away and leaving you to this walk. A charm for doubt. A charm against Trump. A charm for faith in other people, even though. A charm for resisting. A charm for the last twigs to drop off your maxi dress, bought in a supermarket, the right weight, the pockets sagging. A charm for your exposure, your hands pressed against the algaed fabric. A charm for the people you walk by to let you pass unaided. A charm against escaped sobs. A charm against bewilderment at another's suffering, a charm for compassion. A charm for autumn light. A charm for the strength to witness the world. A charm against Neo-Nazis. A charm for the way past the processions of men. A charm for the way through the days of demagogues. A charm for making a lie apparent, a truth evident, a lie scaled and upended. A charm against powerlessness. A charm against the fact that magic does not exist. A charm against power, a charm that has no power, but. A charm for the corner shop and all who sail in her. A charm for a plant in a window with dust on it, and a small cat who sees you and opens its mouth. A charm against consuming as feeble rejoinder to a sense of powerlessness. A charm for living. A charm for the living. A charm for all the lives that will have to resist. A charm for knowing history. A charm for seeing which side blood is buttered. A charm for autumn light. A charm for crossing the road without getting hit. A charm for all Cassandras. A charm for walking away from the end. A charm for gentleness. A charm for the fight. A charm for the air, a charm written on air, and rewritten and always needing to be rewritten. A charm for every day. A charm against despair, and when it does come, for despair splitting like a frayed cord and sparking itself out to leave what is left, a cold feeling, less than content but fit to be retooled to other better use. A charm for autumn light. A charm for the room you left. A charm against the room you left. A charm for the two worlds online and irl and more in which we live what is, and what we think it is. A charm for a lighter and a heavier heart. A charm against a hopeless future. A charm for frailty and continuing to fight. A charm for the world as it is, and your continuing to live in it.

THE LAST OF
THE FAITHFUL

The vestal virgin splashes her bottle of Shalimar, laughing, on the ashes of the fire. Life! Blue-green flames dancing up, and the smell of it, the bergamot, the cracked vanilla, the orchid pods crickling through each cubic inch of the room. She's been out all night, but no worries, darling match-mother, she's home in time. Modern Rome around her coolly just the same, with life and late night floristry, smiles across the bar that she'd slipped from, just at the last gasp. She knows the fire and its whims. Flicking a silver lighter between her fingers. She knows the penalties for letting it go out. *How cute to be in charge of everything*, one man had said. *Martini?* Clipped, assured like that, passing it over into her hands. She felt pretty sure he was some sort of celebrity. A cold extinguishing wind blows harder from a handsome face.

There are not many left of the saviours of the city. Just her, until she can recruit more. Too many women think 'virgin' means what later ages would have you believe. The keeper of the hearth just needs to abstain, for now, from those inside the boundaries of Rome. These virgins are the fire queens of the city. That force of lifeblood, fire, the membranes around a flickering soul that keep it fluid and together. Maybe not so much as in former days, but still, here, she keeps the hearth in the temple, and the temple keeps Rome lit, in all the many ways. To let in a Roman (temporary or otherwise) to her bed is just about incest. Of course a man must have written those rules. Even the image makes no sense.

Outside in the forum raindrops slight the great and ancient brass doors of the senate. No one is there now, talking trash about the city-state, the state of the people's bread. The vestal virgin wanders the brick halls of the House of the Vestals, touching sacred objects to free them from the confines of their stillness. In the bar she had seen the man look at her, with that same touch anticipatory and blatant in his eyes. He did not know her. And would not.

The smell of perfume follows her back to her bedroom. All those white tucked beds, and no one in them. Things used to get quite dramatic, back when the wheat was all here. Stories of guardianship, stories of seduction. All faith is, is a story, a flame passed on between sisters. It has lasted so long, this order, through sacking and fall, through Papal States and Mussolini – some would say the rot started there, when one virgin was inhumed for refusing his groping hands at a ritual of the Argei on the Tiber. But there have been as many scandals as there have been seasons, many frailties, many dropped embers and terrible fiery consummations. The city endured, so the Vestals must too. This last one leaned her head in her hands. A pillow of lavender, a blanket of white fleece. Only a little while, and someone would come to the temple door to pick up the first firestarters of the morning, for the braziers in public buildings. Plain as buying the first coffee of the morning, except that there was no money, only honour. There is ever honour, until there is none.

There it was, the knock. Bleery, still dressed to the nines, she tottered into the chamber of the temple and from the great hearth raised out a burning stick. Opened the door on the rain-washed street. There he was, the man with fame wrapped round him, keeping him bright and healthy and warm. He had come for fire, and its extinguishing. The Vestal narrowed her eyes: and turning away, swung the door on the temple wide, to let him enter in.

THE EXPECTATION OF
A JOB WELL DONE

A curious state of affairs, Ausweiger thought as the men drove him through the desert towards their destination. The flat drab countryside stuttered by, dun sand marked with dark rocks. The surface of Mars it might as well have been. Ausweiger couldn't feel the sun but he soon would. The car took a hard right, going down a barely-defined track between two dun, yes, and rocky hills. They drove for a few more minutes and Ausweiger, looking at his bald reflection in the window pane, did his best to keep his thoughts trim and careful. At last the car stopped, and the men got out. They were in a concave spot in the desert, a place that could have been either natural or unnatural. Seats had been arranged around the highest part of the bowl, and beyond the car, in the very centre, had been placed a large tin bath.

"Ah, all right, okay," said Ausweiger under his breath. The men climbed the hill to their seats, and soon others were beside them, appearing over the crest, having walked out of the desert like phantoms. Ausweiger proceeded to the bath. He pushed the plug into the plughole and ran both taps at full. From the taps came the thin substance that looked almost like water with a pretty, greenish tint. It could have been marsh water, he thought, from the place where he had grown up, a land of huge ferns and tiny white houses. Reflections from the liquid danced around the sides of the bath and on Ausweiger's face. He began to meticulously remove his clothes, starting with the shoes and working up, leaving his boxers on because even here he was shy.

His little paunch, with its line of fine dark hair, was looking less protruding, he thought. Even now, he had such thoughts.

The bath was about half-way full. Ausweiger lifted one foot, his left, and hovered it over the liquid. The men viewing from the hill had their black hats low on their faces, or else sunglasses. They said nothing, did not break the silence at all, as Ausweiger lowered his foot and the acid began to froth around it, eating the flesh away.

Ausweiger lifted the leg up, now a stump with a single, stripped bone remaining. He clapped some dust from his hands.

"Now which?" he called.

A pause came, and then one man said, "Right Arm." There was a quiet and general sense of agreement at this, but Ausweiger frowned. He made little theatricality of this dip, and when the handless arm came back out, he shook off the drops and turned to the men again.

"I will next lie down," he said.

"Fair," said the man who had spoken before. In such crowds, there will be one who finds the voice of all and speaks it.

Ausweiger manoeuvred himself into the bath, leaning on his good left hand. He held his breath, though even then thinking, what a thing to do. The acid rose up around him in a great hissing roiling mass. He sank into it, and lay down so that first the back of his head, then his whole head, was submerged. The sky was above him and full of an infinity that had no use for finite creatures such as Ausweiger. It was then that the bath, the sand, and his body began to fall back, and in the process of falling, begin to re-assemble from the acid-broken particles and their memory of being Ausweiger's flesh and bones. There was a rushing, screaming wind and a flickering blue. The tin bath spun out, and Ausweiger, as he became other than the Ausweiger he had been in all his days thus far, swore he heard it clatter off in the distance, where other old spent things had gathered, collecting dust.

A VOICE SPOKE
TO ME AT NIGHT

I don't know why it did. I live in a new-build above a Tesco
Metro. This part of town seems to be historyless; I think
before they built the flats there was an auto garage and before
that I don't know, maybe something brownfield. But the voice
that spoke to me was from someone from years and years in
the past – I guessed, because I didn't fully understand it. I read
a bit of Chaucer in school, and it reminded me of that, a little
bit gibberish and some I could get. The voice had a Scottish
character to it, though not like any dialect I could pick out. On
the first night and for two nights after it was just a voice.

I went to bed at the normal time for me, which is about ten,
and took my phone into bed and scrolled through the news and
some football sites I like and Twitter until I was too tired to read
straight, and then listened to a podcast about a crime and then
one about food, to calm me down.

I like to be cosy with all the blankets around me, especially
my feet, because I have a terrible fear that something will come
and drag me by the ankles if I leave them exposed. This and the
mirrored sliding doors of my built-in wardrobe are two things
which unsettle me when I'm trying to sleep. I never liked the
empty space of the mirrors taking up so much of my room,
even before this happened. Now I can't stop thinking of them,
everything a mirror is, and everything it isn't. I am trying to be
honest here. I'm not a brave type.

I had just put down my phone and got into the position I find comfy in bed – left-hand side, curled up, pillow against my stomach – when the voice said – something. Garbled old language coming across a distance. I held my mouth shut so I wouldn't yell, but of course I knew it could have come from anywhere, that voice, the likely culprit being my phone, which I might have left in the bed and rolled over, setting off some video. I put the light on and found my phone – it was on silent But the voice had also stopped. I didn't think anything too much of it; I had lots of reasons to soothe myself with. If not the phone, then the downstairs or next door neighbour's TV echoing through the walls as they watched some documentary about the ancient past.

After a while of thinking, I slept, and then woke up. I went about my day fine enough; I had a meeting with my boss, but it was okay. He doesn't think much of me – he doesn't hate me either, since I do what needs doing and I don't complain. If I don't join in with workplace bonding, chatting about the telly and politics and that, then that's all he can hold against me, and it's not enough to make him want to let me go, I tell myself.

I went home at the usual time and tried to wait out the usual unpleasant feelings that I get from meetings with my boss. I just ate toast for dinner. Sometimes toast is the limit. I went to bed and decided to read, but I got distracted from my book and picked up my phone and looked at Tinder, but only because I wanted to look at some faces, not to make any decisions.

I went to sleep, and this time the voice woke me up, clearer and closer. I should say it was a man's voice, slightly gruff and raspy, like he smoked, but I'm pretty sure the time he's supposed to be from they didn't have tobacco. That was Francis Drake. Tobacco and the potato.

The voice didn't sound urgent, I thought. But you can't always read tone in a voice that you don't expect, coming out of nowhere in the middle of the night, and barely in your language. I checked my phone, I turned all the lights in the place on. There was nothing. The voice continued for a while, so I decided with a bit of effort it was either the neighbours or maybe, maybe a spy, whose equipment had malfunctioned and now their bug in my place was throwing back the sound of him talking while reading out a very old story in old time Scots, because he was bored. I quite liked that idea, and wished him well, that spy, if he was so low down on the list of spy-employees that his job was spying on me.

Eventually I slept. When I woke up, it had decided to become Autumn overnight. I don't like Autumn because it does the usual and makes me a bit sad without specific reasons, just when I'm trying my best.

When it comes I know the year is getting old, and soon it will be over, another year, and I don't have any particular thoughts about that, except I feel vaguely anxious. As if that's not enough, the leaves that get everywhere make me think of slipping and hurting myself, and the darkness makes me worry I will slip and hurt myself on the leafy ground and go unseen, because everyone else is indoors, safe, with their curtains closed against the darkness, which has swallowed me up, and after a while, even the streetlights go out because in my imagination they are activated by motion, and then I just lie there. But I like to imagine I'd be brave while lying there, if I am not knocked out.

The rain threatened all day but never came, which is just typical of Autumn. I walked home catching up with my phone but stepping very carefully between the leaves, because there's no point being careless, if you have the energy to be careful. You have to take care of yourself. The clouds looked heavy and did nothing with their rain, while the leaves hung on the city trees by their edges. It was like they were waiting until night came properly down before letting go and making the pavement even more treacherous, but beautiful too, I suppose, in their jaggy layers. There's always something beautiful going on, which I should try to notice and remember.

This time the voice came while I was eating my dinner and watching a Let's Play of a kingdom-building game. I knew the voice wasn't from that, because I'd heard all the sounds of that game, which were mostly upbeat bleeps, and the voice of the let's player, which was Canadian and silly.

The voice, the strange old voice, spoke to me this time with a bit more neediness, I think, and it kept on going. But I didn't say anything, because what could I say? Saying something would be acknowledging it was there, and I was trying to believe it was just a fluke of sounds from harmless places, the thin walls, some devices malfunctioning, and holding on to the fact, I thought, that it wasn't me malfunctioning. Though how would I know? The voice rambled on, raspy and dry and a little bit wobbly. I could hear some emotion other than need – like he needed to know I was listening, but also that the story he was telling was something that was painful to him and important. I could have got more of what he was saying if I listened closer, but I didn't want to do that.

What could I do? I went to bed and put my headphones in. Eventually the voice, which never got any louder, started to hesitate, and then stopped.

When I woke up the next day I remembered it was a Saturday. I was nervous about staying all day in my flat, with that voice potentially coming back at any moment, but I also didn't want to change my plans for what was possibly a kind of hallucination on my part, so I stayed in and made French toast. Anyway it was raining, properly lashing it down. Like God was angry with pavements and streets and was trying to pummel them back into muddy ground again. I ate the French toast with ketchup and looked at my phone at a few videos of *Hearthstone*, which if you don't know is a card-based computer game that's free-to-play and has a bit of a look of pinball machine to it, only with magical cards.

I had just had a shower – it was four pm – when I walked into my bedroom and saw a man in the mirrored sliding door.

He was looking away. You do not know how disconcerting it is to see the back of someone's head in the mirror, right where you are standing. You can never see the back of your own head facing a mirror like that, and to see someone else's is sickening. I think I shouted, because the man in the mirror seemed to flinch, and then turned round.

My first and strongest thought was that I should run away, but I just stood and stared at the man there. He had a thin, skeletal face, but ruddy in the cheeks, like someone who had worked outside a lot and was healthy, but didn't have much food to eat. He had thin, fine hair that lay on the top of his head in sharp points. It was the kind of grey hair people are born with, I don't know a name for the colour, but it's common enough. I remember his fingers going up to his head to straighten the hair in place as he looked at me. He had deeply set eyes pale back there in his skull. He moved like no one else I've ever seen. It must have been his lack of body fat. He sort of slink-stepped closer to the glass and put his hand up to that. There was sky, grey clouds behind him like he was standing on the top of a hill. I started to shudder as I was breathing, quick and shallow breaths, and my whole body trembling.

"Nolit timere," he said. He said it a few times over the course of the night, and later I looked it up. It means do not be afraid, in Latin. But I nearly started wailing. Maybe I did, I don't remember. Maybe I barked like a dog. I had known before he spoke that he was the owner of the voice I had been hearing, but it didn't make it any less terrifying and upsetting to have that proved true. I was either mad, or I wasn't mad, and both options were fucking awful. I backed out of the room and slammed the door behind me.

I went to the kitchen and downed a glass of very acidic orange juice and splashed water on my face. I went to the toilet and had a long piss and washed up and brushed my teeth. I went back to the room, because it was my room, and I hoped he would have gone, but of course he was still there, staring out at me from his thin face that had the cheek to look concerned. Eventually, since nothing was going to stop any of this from happening to me, I got together myself and put on some kind of unified front.

"Who are you?" I asked. "What's your name?"

I pointed to my chest, and said my name. "And you?"

"Name? Nomen?" he said. I nodded.

He said his name, but it was an old one, and I didn't know it, and I couldn't repeat it if I tried. Mal-something. Not Malcolm, but close. I might know it again if someone said it out loud, but I don't think that's likely to happen. I'm giving this as kind of evidence that I didn't hallucinate him, because if I had, I probably would have made up a name I could remember. Even my subconscious would have. I'm not that creative, and I know a lot of names, generally, from all kinds of eras of history, and I've read a lot of fantasy books. But I didn't know his, so I didn't really catch it and I don't remember it now.

"What are you doing in my mirror?" I asked. He looked around and held out his hands. I noticed the fingers were long, and I thought that was surprising because if he was from some time way back in the dark ages he probably would be considered very tall. He was even a little taller than I am, and I'm average for nowadays, with all the food and vitamins and modern medicines we have.

"Okay," I tried. "What are you doing here? Why do you keep coming here? Do you know where you are? You're in my house. In my bedroom." I didn't want to say, that's pretty rude of you, but my tone probably implied it. I put my hands on my hips, but took them off right away. Just because he was in my house didn't mean I had to be a knob. And technically he wasn't in my bedroom; he was in the mirror, or the place that could be seen through my mirror, with heavy clouds moving quickly, like the ridge of a hill. He took a small shuddery breath in, just like one of my breaths from earlier, and began his story. It was in a mixture of Scots and some Latin, and I made him stop a bit so I could press record on my phone. Later, I played it back and worked out what he had said, which took a long time.

He told me he was the only man left alive in his village. He tried to describe where his village was, but I didn't recognise it from the names of the hills he mentioned. He did say it was half a day's walk from the sea, though that doesn't cut much out in this country. You're never more than about forty miles from the sea in Scotland. A plague had come and made everyone ill but him, over a period of a few weeks. And then everyone started dying. He talked a lot about bodies, how they had stacked up everywhere in the huts and he couldn't keep up with burying, but he had tried his best. He mentioned God a lot. That was a word I recognised when he spoke, Deus. I nodded when I heard it; he said it with a lot of pain.

He said he went into every house and that death was inside each one, standing over the bodies with her long soft wings. Yes, just like that he said it, and I shivered when I worked out the translation. He talked about the grain rotting in the field; he had been trying to get it all in for the winter. He said his hands bled from effort, and he hoped that I would believe him that they bled from effort, and not think he had just given himself an easy life. He mentioned a flour mill, and said he had gone there with the grain piled up on the laird's horse – I don't know who the laird was – but there was no one attending the mill, and he had tried to grind the grain but didn't do a good job of it. So he went home. And he ran out of hope, he said, and had no one left to bury but everyone left to cry for, and nothing much else to do with his days except feel his heart's pains and put what food away for the winter that he could.

He had decided to live in the laird's house because it was off from the village and had had the least visits from death, even though, he said, it was a sin to take the laird's place. He sighed and shuddered a lot here, so clearly it worried him, what he'd done – he wanted to reassure me he didn't have any ideas about his station in life suddenly being raised above what was natural.

He said he had learned to read from a brief stay with some monks as a boy. Here I was a bit confused, something to do with almost becoming a young monk but his father needed him and pulled him out, and it had caused some bother, but he was his father's only child, or had become his only child, so they let him go. It had broken his heart, because he had loved learning, and the monastery life was not supposed to be something you just left. He felt it was his sins that had led him out of the path to knowledge, he said, though he was just a boy then and his sins were only small ones. His father had had to pay something for taking him out, sheaves of oats, I think, for some years. He had wondered if leaving the monastery was the reason why the angel of death hadn't come for him, if it was a kind of curse, and he wanted to find out.

In the laird's house there was a library of books, and he spent some time reading, which he had never before been able to do. He built a fire up very high but made sure to replace the wood every day, in case someone came and threw him out. But no one came. He stayed up late in the evenings and read lots of the laird's Latin books, and there was a Greek one that interested him but gave him some trouble until he found an alphabet for it in the children's room upstairs. The children were dead too, he said. Everyone was dead.

So in the empty house he taught himself Greek and how to read better. He wanted me to know he used his time well and wasn't idle. He found nothing that said it was a sin to be taken out of a monastery so he thought perhaps when the plague would pass and people returned he might make another attempt to enter the monastery with his new learning and make his life a kind of careful atonement for his sins, his other sins in life, though he couldn't think exactly what they were, perhaps sins of the mind. He was someone who thought a lot, it seemed. But then, he'd had lots of time to think about things.

I don't think I would have known what to do in that situation, if everybody around me died. Possibly I wouldn't know until I needed to go to the shops for something. I'd be fine until the food in the shops spoiled, and the electricity went out, then I'd be in some trouble. But this man kept himself going, he said, for a whole turn of the seasons, a year. All alone, with nobody coming. Could I have gone on too, like he had? Realistically I would have just died of starvation quite quickly because I can't support myself in any practical way.

When I was writing out what he'd said, after the mirror had gone back to normal, I wished I could have asked him questions in real time.

I wanted to know if he had a wife, and I wasn't clear on how a peasant like him with no more than a few months' education could teach himself a whole other language. I wanted to tell him I was impressed by that. I wanted to tell him too that I was sorry he was so alone in his world.

Loneliness is a terrible thing, wherever you are. I think it's a stronger force than love, because it's a kind of love for everyone that is never returned. In that way, maybe it's not so terrible but a kind of burning power that might give you something back, if you have it in you, beaming out. I'm not the kind of person to run away with conspiracy theories, but I can't help but feel like the reason he could see me, across the years like that, and really improbably, was because of the force of his loneliness, making a portal or something.

I don't know why he should connect with me out of anyone in existence ever. I'm not very interesting, or powerful, in my day-to-day life or in my imagination. I'd be the last to get picked for a special mission to save the earth and the first to die in a magical world, a random casualty trampled by a beast or army, I know that much. But I keep going, and now I keep going knowing that he came to me. Maybe everyone has a visit from a lonely person from the past through their mirrors; I wouldn't be surprised. I'd like the world a bit better if that was the case.

After he had finished speaking, I went up to the mirror and tried to push through it, but that didn't work. He also tried, but gave up and shook his head. Then I remembered it was a good thing I couldn't go in, because I'd read that the microbes I have on my skin have evolved a lot since the microbes on his skin were in existence, meaning that I might be a source of disease myself, if I came into contact with him, and probably the other way round too. But who knows how it works; maybe the mirror would have cleansed me or covered me with a protective layer like a spacesuit. But I couldn't get through and he couldn't get through. I sat down, and he did too. The wind on his side ruffled his fine hair and he pulled his woollen clothing close around him. I knew he couldn't sit there forever. I thought I could.

I had such a funny feeling in my heart, even then, when I hadn't known everything he'd said. I nursed that feeling, and I looked at him for a long time saying nothing. He looked back at me. I wondered what he was looking into. Mirrors weren't very common in the dark ages, or whenever there were peasants around. I guessed maybe it was the glass window of the laird's house. I went and got a piece of printer paper and scribbled out my idea of his set up. A big house with him sitting on the grass outside it. He shook his head, and made some shapes in the air, jagged. I think he meant the glass was in a big piece lying against something, a tree maybe.

I wondered how he got the idea to look in the glass. I wondered a lot of things, just sitting there, looking at him, with my bed behind me. I wanted to invite him through into my house and put him up. He could have the bed. I'd have done anything for him. That face of his, it was a good face, honest and thin. Lots of cares written on it.

I stared for so long, sometimes smiling and raising my hand, like an idiot really, but I didn't know what else to do.

Eventually it started getting dark on his side. I turned and saw from my window it was getting dark too. The light faded, and he faded, and I couldn't see him anymore. I cried out, just something pointless like 'hey! I can't see you anymore!' And he said something back, calmer than me. I didn't get a chance to record it. I don't usually get gut feelings about much, but I felt certain I wouldn't see him again, or at least not for a long time. His face comes back to me, in waves, I see it, kind, and wanting, getting. I wonder what he thought about my face, if he liked it. It must have looked strange to him, soft and unfamiliar, but I hope he thinks for all that, that it was a good face too, that my company was good for him, after so much time alone.

THIS PLACE IS MINE

So I woke up one morning to my own house changed around me, to find the soot fallen in the fallen down chimney, a set of tiny feline bones on what had been the rug, and now was nothing but a mouldered scrap, but I felt so rested, so glorious. It was the light, you see. It's always the light that buoys us. No matter the damp papers, the rot in the heart of the books. There are stories that lash themselves to us without words. There are stories that travel down every line of light.

I went to pick up the phone, and the cord came away in my hand, and the hall stand it was on collapsed with the sudden movement. No words for me. I laughed until my throat burned. The sound of pigeons fluttering like pinwheels drew me up into the attic. I knew before looking that there was no glass in the windows, or in any of the windows on the street. It is funny how much you laugh when you know you are doomed, but the manner of your damnation turns out to be so calm, so precisely your own. I stood on a rusty nail, and pulled it out just as easily.

What they would tell me later is that I had slept. They would try to tell me more of it, and every time I'd put my hand up, laughing, until they stopped talking, and listened to me. Their dirty, thin, modern faces turned up to mine. I was the old world and its disgraces. I was the thing to be seen and marvelled at, to project my understanding of what was lost. No more recording every moment now – all cameras broken, all blood red batteries leached to spitting shells.

I had no reason to feel ashamed. I carried my ruination out of that house as I had brought it primly indoors. Each day I left the sleepers to their rest – I never would again – and sat light and watchful over camp and the now distant blue-shadowed city stuffed with leathered bones and rust, and searched until I saw my old house, an eyeless mirror, set just so.

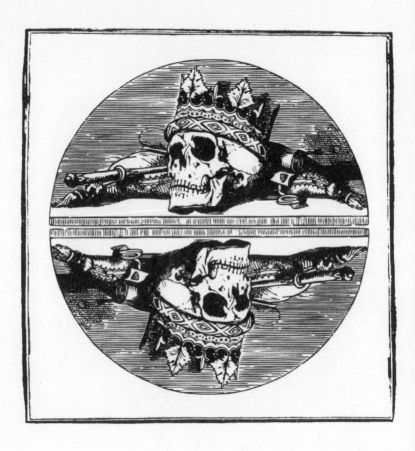

WHAT CAN BE
ENDURED MAY YET
BE UNBEARABLE

Here is the main boulevard, tree-lined and still; and in the elegant residential buildings lining the boulevard, the thoughtless are asleep, the news having come yesterday to no riots, no sound of objection at all. But in the fourteenth building, up on the fourth floor, third window along, I have not forgotten it. The cup of coffee on my desk is six days stale, so what? A great deal of the universe has grown cold.

In the kitchen there is a little blood on the tiled floor and my dog is missing, having snuck out by the door left ajar. Someone knocks. *Delivery! Pizza and roses!* he says, with a tight flourish, producing both from behind his back. I take them and walk back inside. He has an unusual accent and dank, long hair that looks like a wig. He sways but is not drunk. *Ma Donna*, he says, still standing there. We gape a while at one another. I have plum-scented votives burning on a wooden chopping board. At the sight of these he claps his hands. I invite him in because it's very possible he is Death.

We sit on the sofa and he pulls all the topping off his pizza slice before eating it. I decide from this irrefutable proof that he must be Death. He rolls up the dough as small as it will go and laughs and pushes it into his mouth. His face is lumpy. Outside I begin to hear sounds of distress from down in the street. Death stands and presses his greasy hands against the window. I look around. There's the cream fleecy blanket. That will do. I pull it around my body like rolling a map, no – a burrito. You don't have to make plans or a future with a burrito. I remove the needle and thread out from their hiding place. X stitches caterpillar up the sides of the casing. Soon I'm clasped safe, with only my head left to the elements, though that won't be for long.

Death has opened the window. The fires have come, probably, and all the lost dogs are dancing on their hind legs. *Hai doggies* Death calls down to the street. But here in my room in my blanket there is quiet, smelling of melted cheese and oregano. Death looks back at me and waves his ineffectual royal wave as I close myself up entirely.

POINTS NORTH

The walk began at midnight. Beforehand, everyone gathered in the community centre adjusting their packs and distributing headlamps, pulling down their woollen hats and tying their laces with as much focus as small children, loop around loop, with their teeth clenched.

All the walkers were women, because none of the men nearby would come. It was a finemilled October night with a white moon hung on it, sculpted and bare of ornament, befitting the hours ahead. At first, the walk took place in silence – just the clinking sounds from lucky carabiners and the rustle of salopettes, and boots on an asphalt road that ran unseen beside the motorway, curving through bottle-strewn brush. There were about fifty women in total and no leader, though some had taken on the role temporarily to bring the people together. The sense of hierarchy shifted in walking. Who was fast and who was slowest, the ones who knew the way. Where they were going required paths that only show themselves at night. Certain trackers are adept at seeing them; with the lenses of their eyes slipped off, they describe lines, parallel lines no wider than dog-tracks, violet-white, wending through open ground like streams seeking the main channel that will hand them to the sea. Perhaps the channels aren't only there at night, perhaps the trackers wanted their companions to be on uneven footing, ready, wary in the dark.

The women walked out of the town and twenty miles onwards, then shifted off across the dead bracken, and up into ice-bitten moor. There was no snow but there was the idea that going quickly would stop the closing-in of the weather. The moon kept hollow watch from a lower point in the sky. A train passes this way, a little further into the moor, in the zero hours after midnight and before dawn. It is never recorded on the timetables, and it makes no stops but two. While the women headed further across the moor it was moving shushed and fleet from the south, stitching through every tungstened city and along the sides of shapeless fields and hills.

On that night, as expected, the violet-white path led up to the isolated station. The women would have to wait for the train to come in, whenever it would. They set up a refreshment stand in the shelter on the platform: water boiling on portable burners, a stack each of plastic cups, teabags, powdered milk, a few to distribute and clean up. All this as quietly as possible, since there was a farmhouse some way behind.

They drank with their headlamps turned down to illuminate hands and avoid burning out the retinas of their neighbours. They sucked down multiple cups, paced the platform or stood carefully at the edge of the lonely track to the farmhouse, holding their cigarettes cupped in their palms in the way of wartime soldiers.

Just as some of the women were beginning to talk of turning back for home, the train was sighted, a tiny light half a mile off. It pulled up slow and ticking at the station, bearing a single carriage that was shuttered, the whole a dark, matte blue like all the night standing behind it. No one in the driver's seat, and through the tall windows of the carriage could be seen the moor, and closer, the reflection of the women on the platform in a line. They went to the doors and pressed for entry. The doors opened. From inside the carriages came a quiet, sharp and keening sound. There was visible a sheen of gold against the dark, a push of bodies receding to make room. A number of the women got on board and let the doors close behind them. The others waited, then at length began the long walk back to their city, silently over the moors and through the underpasses.

Meanwhile the train proceeded northwards with additional cargo. At a station to the far north-west, right at the brink where the cliffs constantly teethe a wild dark sea, on tracks half buried by the heather, the train, with ponderous slowness, terminated. The platform here was little more than a clearing, and the descent from the train was slow and careful. One by women the women stepped out, hauling their loads of bags and boots. They formed a queue and looked up at the train. They were tired, yes, but full. Nothing but a drip of gold liquor remained on board the train, running a puddle like mercury from the back of the carriage to the vestibule.

Across the tracks they located the row of cottages where they would wash and brush the gold out of their drab hair, gathering flecks to save for gifts for those who had been left behind. And there in the cottage, they set a fire, sat in the amber of the unfamiliar room and whispered what they had done that the men would never do, and what it had done to them they did not yet know. Their speech frantic at first, then slowing, easing, the more they spoke. Gold around their mouths scrubbed clean, now, but stains illuminated the gaps between their teeth. An unholy feast had occurred, the kind that ritual demands, and after granted the kind of power a ritual bestows, and some dulling elevation and binding, and the women felt themselves changed by it. They pinched the webbing between their fingers, stroked their nails thoughtfully along their throats. And underneath, or the idea of underneath, their skin was unable to glitter because there was so little light, now, the light having been talked out of those throats.

When it grew late, knowing home awaited in the morning, but that there were many hours until then, many openings possible, the women clambered into bunks with the golden chains left there on them, raised the chains and put them about their bodies, and locked themselves down at the edge of the world.

THE COMPANION

The inside of the tent had a beautiful glow to it, a buttery yellow. It was part of the reason Louisa had chosen it for her trek. Going out alone, she reasoned, it would be good to have this bit of colour to look forward to at the beginning and end of each day. This was morning and time for lard cake and waiting for the snow to melt for coffee, and calling home, and looking at the compass and the maps, then the less-fun tasks of packing up the canoe, checking the kit was secure, and making the blood sigil to ward off the polar bear who had been following her trail these past three nights. She said nights, still, even though there was no darkness, just a switch to pink or lavender in the sky at around midnight.

The needle of the compass twitched. Louisa could taste coffee vapours crystalising on the inside of her face mask, and heard the sound of her skis and her poles scraping across the disruption of the sea ice. At this time of day, the risk of attack was minimal, and all she had was that noise, that taste, the treachery beneath, and the cold air around. The cold was one of the reasons she had come. It was dull to say it made her feel alive, but Louisa had trouble finding the right words around what it did do to her. It blasted some alchemical joy, made her veins fizz and her eyes bright. Each slog of a day, prior to realising she was being tracked, had been brilliantly rewarding.

If there was a way to hold onto that thread of goodness.

If there was a way to keep the broadness of the arctic indifferent to her.

If there was a way to be a witch, even if she had only so far learned one solitary, useless spell.

Going back was the easiest option, and Louisa was no fool. But. She continued, and walked the days. For the next four nights the polar bear circled her golden tent. She began daubing the blood sigils before sleep – at a distance. Writing blood on sift ice is hard work, but when they began to glow, something would settle inside and she would sleep despite the noise. That rattle at the bear's throat, a wheeze of the kind with which an old woman might be afflicted, or the whirring down of clockwork. That too, when Lousia did hear it edging on her sleep, gave her grim hope.

It was about three o'clock, judging by the sun, when she saw the hulking mass of the bear ahead of her at rest on a piled wave. She saw its yellow fur hung low on its body. Skin loose, and starving under it. It is not hard to be outpaced even by a sickly polar bear, nor are appointments with death in the arctic ever truly unexpected. There was no diverting from her course, unless she got into her canoe and paddled, and even then the gap in the floes looked likely enough to close up, trapping her. So Louisa walked. She took out her compass, looked at the wavering needle begin to turn, the iron growing frantic as the distance between her and the white bear lessened. Still Louisa did not discount her own survival, yet.

Walking towards the bear, she thought about herself as a presence in this space, blocked off from free movement by her own heavy clothes. If she was a primal figure it was that of hubris, of course. The bear was hunger, the kind of goddess figure no religion in human history has ever prayed to, only to escape. Hunger, need. Black eyes and panting, wheezing mouth full of long yellow teeth

She was about twenty metres away. Below the beast stretched a black pool in the ice, scattered with something red. Louisa clenched her hand where the sigil cuts itched. In a land without reference, spells will sometimes fail. That's what home had said. She whispered to herself, a prayer this time: *what*. Ski step over ski step is slow going, but eventually the black, red-filled pool rose to a lake. The polar bear sat breathing with the familiar wheeze, mouth open, staring at her. Louisa moved closer. There came the chalky crick of the ice, but the edge of the black lake seemed stable for the moment, for the both of them. It struck her that the reason her own breath came steadily was that there were too many competing opportunities for her death.

Red things moved in the water: they were being nudged aside by more and more small bulbous shapes blipping up crimson from the black depths.

Louisa pulled back her hood and took off her face mask. The polar bear made a huffing, rasping sound. She turned to it again to see it stand and pull back its head, looking up, looking down at her, looking at the pool, in which floated – roses. A conjured fleet of heart-red rose heads, each open, almost overblown. Louisa could not run to any purpose, so knelt to gather them from the water, and under the continued watch of the bear, a pile of flowers amassed. Though her fingers were numb it seemed to her that she could still feel their petals, impossibly soft, and that even when they lay on the ice they were soft, and smelled like the Turkish delights she loved as a child, dusted with icing sugar. Louisa took her gloves off, thinking of the damage, but mostly of the miraculous. The polar bear came to the pile. It nosed them first, then began eating. So Louisa picked up a red bloom and ate it too. Velvet and tender.

Louisa lay down beside the roses. The bear lay down, still now and then licking up a blossom and chewing it noisily. Together they waited, curled. Louisa thought: to be given the inexplicable alongside death. And also: this seems then the whole package of dying, like the dying in a painting. But there wasn't an objectivity that took it on itself to answer. The scarcity around their opulent centre creaked white. Her scarred, slowly freezing hand reached, over and over, into the same festivity. Long, yellow teeth, petal-covered tongues, sweet breath. Something, something, was going to break.

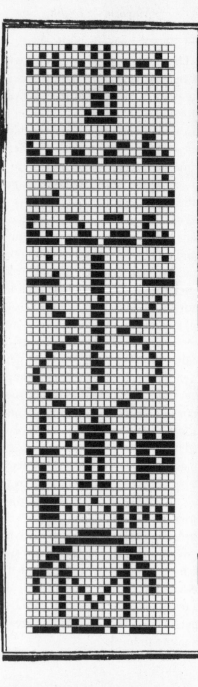

TAKE CARE, I LOVE YOU

Sections in bold are taken from the contents for the Wikipedia article on the Fermi Paradox, which examines the contradiction between mathematical probability that suggests alien life should exist in our universe and the lack of any evidence that it does.

5   Hypothetical explanations for the paradox
A poem about loneliness

5.1   Extraterrestrial life is rare or non-existent
You wonder about other people

5.2   No other intelligent species have arisen
They seem to manage and group together

5.3   Intelligent alien species lack advanced technology
You stare at your phone to keep the room from collapsing

5.4   It is the nature of intelligent life to destroy itself
You're not sure how smart or stupid you are, it's going along okay, mostly

5.5   It is the nature of intelligent life to destroy others
At work you offer your colleague a mince pie but they are distracted

5.6   Periodic extinction by natural events
You take your time walking around the supermarket, it is bright and busy

5.7   Inflation hypothesis and the youngness argument
You play *Witcher 3* when you get home for six hours and it's much more beautiful than real life

5.8   Intelligent civilizations are too far apart in space or time
You can go on holiday by yourself, that's fine, you're saving up for Italy in the new year

5.9   It is too expensive to spread physically throughout the galaxy
Your mum said she was glad you were doing so well

5.10   Human beings have not existed long enough
It's so hard to know what to do

5.11   We are not listening properly
You're not able to tell anyone

5.12   Civilizations broadcast detectable radio signals only for a brief period of time
You like the idea of Snapchat, but there's nobody who'd do it with you

5.13   They tend to isolate themselves
The last time you broke down and actually talked to your mum about how you feel all the time she said 'where did I go wrong?'

5.14   They are too alien
You might look for a new job, you might fit in better somewhere else

5.15   Everyone is listening, no one is transmitting
You check your texts even so

5.16 Earth is deliberately not contacted

Of course you're going to say 'it's all my fault' because you always make it about you

5.17 Earth is purposely isolated (planetarium hypothesis)

Looking out the window at the old man tottering along on the icy pavement with his wee dog, wondering if he has a family

5.18 It is dangerous to communicate

You very nearly told the cashier 'take care, I love you', and you'd have meant it

5.19 The Simulation Theory

It has to be better than this

5.20 They are here undetected

You've joined Twitter but you don't really know how it works, you're trying

5.21 They are here unacknowledged

In your new profile you've just put what seemed right: take care, I love you.

OVERWINTERNIGHT

Christmas Eve finds you sitting alone in a bothy on the side of the mountain in the Scottish Highlands, soaked to your underwear, poking at damp logs and trying to get a fire to catch. It's taken you all day to get here, though it was not at first a strenuous journey. This is a families-and-their-dogs type of summit, busy most holidays and weekends in good weather. The hut is only provided on the off-chance of bad weather and foolishness, which there are plenty of in this instance.

The day started out blue and frosty. You dawdled, ate snacks, took breaks to cry into your sleeves when there was no sign of other walkers. Towards noon, a sudden turn. Sleet and driving rain, to the point where people were muttering on their way back down, turn back, pal, it's not going to let up tonight. But dreich was what you needed. Any excuse to put your head down and trudge onwards. Whatever was it possessed you, at the summit, to leap down off a last rock, like you were someone with a need to be leaping? Then over on the ankle, the pain stratospheric. You rub the swelling. Not serious; pathetic, mostly, in the pantheon of bodily injury. And leaving a dull throb; you hold that throb to yourself like a gift. True you could have louped down the mountain on your good leg, or caved and called for help. But you have your reasons.

Somewhere in a secret pocket there's one of Jamie's lighters. It takes a while to locate, while you shiver open the rucksack's knots and zips. You'd love a nip of something, something brash and peaty and warming, though you don't drink, you remind yourself. What else? No lantern, no sleeping bag, not much in the way of food. A gritty packet of soup and some old teabags from another trip. No pot or stove to coax the worth from them. There though, the fire's catching. You get to work on your damp boots and your wet socks, then rub at your slab-cold feet. After an hour, misery ebbs, and you take the measure of everything around. In the firelight you can make out dirt floor, doorless cupboards, log basket, rough ladder up to the sleeping loft. You won't be sleeping up there, not with your ankle the way it is, and so far from the only heat.

There's a sharp knocking at the door – who knocks at a bothy? It's meant for all comers. You wince over, getting your feet clarty. At the door, there's nothing. Winter dark and its stars in a weatherless sky. The barely visible windsheltered side of the hill in the soft light from the windows. Then, there's a large white owl. It is standing right in front of you, looking up.

You've never seen an owl in the wild before, not alive anyway. You don't even know if this country is in their usual range. Certainly this high up on a mountain seems unlikely, even if it is, judging by the plumage, a winter-adapted owl. Plumage, as if you even know a thing about owls. What species is this? It's very large actually, almost the size of a toddler, though that implies something weak and awkward. You are, it's true, unsure of owls in general. You are the awkward one here. You hop to one side, and the owl walks in. Perhaps it has a broken wing, is disorientated. It moves to the fire, and jumps onto one of the wooden benches. You close the door and slowly seat yourself back down where you were. The owl gives you a friendly glare. Eyes like amber in a hunched mottled body. Nothing happens. For some time, you both sit watching the fire, which smokes and crackles. You wriggle your toes at the grate, and then stop, in case the owl is offended, or mistakes them for baby mice.

Eventually your eyes grow weary, and you pull on your dried socks and stretch out on the bench, mindful of the creature beside you. As you sleep you dream brilliantly of the large white owl. In the dream, the owl, grown larger still, removes its coat and balaclava of feathers. Under it all is a squat-necked woman, or a man, or a child of any gender – you can't be sure, still with the same terrible pitiless owl-eyes. The owl-person, still seated by the fire, takes out a set of knitting needles and begins to tick away on them.

You want to ask something, but if there's anything worth asking, the heat of the fire and your reluctance to break silence hides the words away in the back of your mouth. Nothing but a sigh escapes, full of ambiguity as sighs always are. Are you content? Stymied? It is not the time to lock your emotions into any particular definition.

At a point before dawn you wake feeling a sudden pressure on your shoulder. You try very carefully not to panic as you realise the weight of owl is upon you. The owl flaps its wings a few times, and the door creaks open. You are sure the owl's head must turn all the way round to check on whoever is here now. You don't have any power of motion, beyond moving your legs, which seems risky. Now you think, what if the owl is insane and attacks you in a frenzy. This presumes owls can go mad. Rabid, then.

The pressure lifts: the owl has hopped down from the post of your person and is walking over to greet the new guest. You get up too. Flurries blithering in. A snowflake lands in your eye, not that there is much to see anyway in the dimness. Water trickles down your cheek. Nothing has come; the door stands open with the owl on the open threshold. And then, in a moment marked by no sound, the bird is gone. You wait, then close the door after. The fire falls in on itself while you sleep, and come the morning you look around, then get to packing, telling yourself not to linger.

You stand at the door now. It's Christmas Day, a day for ambiguities and sharp joy. You allow yourself that belief, alone of all others. Whiteness spreads soft below, as far and far as you can see.

POWDERED MILK

A novella

For the lost

Blessed are the dead that the rain rains upon:
But here I pray that none whom once I loved
Is dying tonight or lying still awake
Solitary, listening to the rain

From 'Rain' by Edward Thomas

"Another," says Maddie, standing at the bank of windows, gripping her mug, her green mug the holy colour of grass. "Another beautiful day." It has been fourteen months since the last supply drop, and most of the crew have gone to the chapel. Smothered, battered, poisoned, starved. Most, but Maddie remains, along with Kaspar, who doesn't count, and Edward and Beaumont, who do. Maddie can feel her joints cracking, and the fine hair all over her body rising in the temperate air. She shivers, and even shivering tires her. It hurts to stand up for too long. Outside the thickness of the window, the vale is lit up for ten metres, but beyond that light, hangs a thick curtain of darkness, suspended forever. In the sliver of light broadcast intentionally for the outside cameras, a world finds a way to exist. A grey world: the particular grey of the trench's massy, lumpen floor, and the slightly different grey of the water itself – strange to think of it as the ocean, having been so completely within it for so long – wrapping around the base, all of this made the more desolate by the noiseless, unending interruption of falling flecks of matter from the world above, marine snow.

"I fucking hate you," Maddie whispers to the thick sweet milk in her cup, eyes resting on nothing, "it's a beautiful day though." She's not mad; she is here, and understanding she is here she takes a drink, and in her mouth the milk swills between her teeth. The dispensary is bare. She thinks of Etan's end, months ago. She hasn't checked on him in a while. Died in his sleep. Edward too is somewhere sleeping, and so is Beaumont. They don't really need the rest, but they can do little else.

A little over fourteen months before, and Johnny was on night disposal duty. Night was established by the base clocks, synched to Chamorro Standard Time, and ran from nine to six. Johnny broke off from his work a little early, coming down to the kitchen and spending one of his rare verbal utterances to complain about having to wrestle a blocked s-pipe.

"It's shit," he said.

"That is very accurate," said Beaumont.

"Man up, kiddo," Charles said from over his paper. "We all have to get into filth every now and then."

"Kiddo. For fuck's sake," said Johnny. He shook himself like a drenched dog, and flicked his hands. "This is the worst."

"Do you have to do that right in the kitchen?" Etan said. Johnny moved to the corner, milking the soap dispenser for the last drops and hosing down his hands and neck with the power spray. Filthy droplets had spattered the cabinets, went rolling into one another and trickling to the floor. The others, even on the common room side, could taste the stink of him in cracks in their lips, in their back molars. Eloise was there too, and Maddie, but neither of them interfered when the men decided to roll on each other.

"Better water pressure at the sink than the showers," Johnny said, grimacing, stripping off his navy overalls along with his day uniform, and folding them in to the washing machine, flinging his industrial gloves in after.

"Liar. Better water pressure outside," said Eloise.

"That's right Johnny, take it *all* off," Edward said.

Charles smirked and threw his paper down on a spot of muck. Johnny tapped the washing to hot and left the room. The laughter broke up, and a hush came down. Then, nothing. Maddie swore she saw something glance by the window, a dingy red sheet draping, for a second, across the space above the trench floor. It was soon gone, out of the sight of the floodlights. A flickering glimpse of some rogue, ruddier type of benthodyte never before catalogued, she thought, though it didn't matter. Not what they were studying, not really, down here, where the biome visible to the eye was meagre, and the microbes this deep had been labelled years ago. No, they were here in this base to study human life contained, far from contact with the external population, and any observations or experiments they ran were mostly to keep them occupied and justify the funding. All this was another dry run for the space colonies, though personally she didn't like the idea of it being a dry run for anything. She believed their project would prove fertile data on the individual versus the communal personality in long term confined spaces, allowing all kinds of insights to be extrapolated, and giving multidisciplinary PhD candidates something to pontificate on for decades to come. Maddie had thought this often, and the thought refreshed her every time. She enjoyed the idea of being a subject, even as she, in point of fact, was the one making the earliest study, the one on the ground taking first-hand readings as the whole project played itself through before her.

Around the common room her colleagues, anticipating the change in shift, were readying themselves and she respected all of them for how earnest they appeared, and how competent, all but Charles, for whom she had, even then, cultivated a dislike. Maddie looked at Charles as he moved on to taking a reading of the mark-three saline charger, and she watched how the others seemed to follow from his lead, turning to their own duties or engaging each other in keen conversations apparently on work topics only after he had committed. She filed this thought away for later, noting which particular member of the crew had responded in what way, however subtle.

Johnny returned to the kitchen pink in the face and his hair wet, and thoroughly wiped down the counters; all was clean again. He had cleaned himself, he spritzed everywhere affected with antibacterial spray, he rinsed that spray off, he dried the surfaces, he folded away the cloth and finally he washed his hands, but nevertheless there had been a lingering feeling of dirtiness that left the evening muted after that point. It was not, as a superstitious person might say, a hint of precognition of what was to come, quite soon. So no one slept well that night in the brightly-lit base – that was simply a matter of a passing collective mood nudged towards watchfulness for no reason. And though it was by the calendar a full moon, you can't blame the moon's influence, that far down in the ocean, even if Etan sometimes tried.

It was, in point of fact that time of the month – supply drop time, which may have added to the tension. There was always a certain anxious feeling in the hours before supplies came in, usually visible in the men more than the women (perhaps simply a cumulative effect, down to how the men outnumbered them seven to three, with Beaumont in their own category). Then, as the carrier docked and was unloaded and sent away, there was a bump, a flood of chatter, morbid jokes. A feeling of bright and hyper very much like emotions attributed to the first steely hours of a full moon. Behind it a primitive feeling, overridden by the rational mind, that the moon would somehow fail to rise, that the food would not be sent down from above to those much in need of it below. As, in fact, it had not, not after that last drop. But there was really nothing remarkable that evening, no matter how much Maddie subsequently remarked on the details of it to herself, turning over in her mind, like anyone might do, those calm hours before it had all started going wrong.

The supply drop was emptied and logged in the usual brisk fashion by Dorothy-Ann and Adam, the nominal quartermasters at that time. The usual crowd had gathered to see what had come in. Seasonal variations and treats included squash, skinless turkey portions, a tub of cinnamon sugar, artisanal butter, mincemeat ice cream in craterous tubs. Some in the crew moaned about the lack of sausage, each taking care not to bring up, again, the superiority of one particular country or region's beloved sausage recipe. Maddie, the vegan, kept her own council on the limited dietary options available to her and the despicable choices of her fellow crew members. She made sure to say she kept them to herself – with an ironic wave – as she picked up the new tee-shirts she had ordered and went for a shower. The day levelled out. Edward and Ben headed to the ROV room to take CURA-UR2Xa (Jelly Bean) for a putter over a quadrant, taking rock measurements and noting if anything living happened to have drifted within range. If they had a can of beer while they tooled about, there was no harm in it. The project allowed for alcohol for those off-shift, but if the work a crew member was doing did not require absolute alertness, no one was going to report a minor violation of the rules. A man needs to get his drink on sometimes, Edward would argue, and the simplicity of that line, its absoluteness, made it true. The Jelly Bean didn't find anything that hadn't already been logged, but Edward and Ben, juggling the controls, did manage to get it to flip over nine times in a row, the highest record of anyone.

The same week of the supply drop, the scheduled relay from CURA'S Guam Base came with a slight delay to it. Then as the head of cooperative subnautics began her introductory remarks, the transmission glitched, warbled. Etan got up from his seat to inspect their connection, with the supervision of Charles, who kept up his usual rapport with both teams. After a while, it wasn't getting any better, so both sides agreed a reschedule for same time the next day. Right before the relay ended, the sound shot up so high in pitch it sounded like the relay team were screaming, and then the screen zipped to black.

The crew reacted calmly. Some paperwork was cleared, the on-shift team went off to their respective workplaces, and then the evening began in earnest.

The common room adjoined the kitchen, and it had been fitted with the largest number of windows in the whole structure: the top half of the wall was covered in them, each pane was about the size of a standard photograph and of a special glass two inches thick to withstand the pressure and more besides, and the panes held by heavy riveted metal strips, as if they might pop off without intense precautions, though they wouldn't, not as long as the crew were there to maintain them. These were the windows where Maddie would later find herself staring outwards, pinned under her own resolve, wondering how many years it would take for them to go, while around her the base hummed and flickered, almost empty.

Back then, on the day the relay had failed, Eloise knocked back the first shot of the hour and began playing violent Spanish guitar over the top of the thrash metal, or whatever it was, that Edward had snuck on, and sang in her strong, deep voice about lives so far gone above them that it would have been sad, had it not been for the comical edge she slid into it, every note drawn out too long. Ben whooped and threw bourbon down his throat, and flipped and caught his glass, a little overdone like always, but harmless with it. So many years they had to be together, no one could be serious all the time, or hold themselves entirely in check.

Maddie tended the bar; contra to her workhour profession-alism she had a free hand. When the crew wanted what they all archly called a shut-in, who was she to fret or raise objections? She could take a drink herself. Dorothy-Ann, a teetotaller, didn't like it much, but she could just go to her bunk. With Adam. Or Trenton. Or both. It was Maddie's job to know who went where with who, and if they had any significant bruises afterwards. Officially, anyone could be cycle through to the role of counsellor, but unofficially, it was always Maddie people came to, to unburden. Given that, of the rest, Charles was the only real alternative – as the only one who had actually been a therapist in a former life – this made sense. But Maddie's judge-mental, chilly remarks would always be delivered from on high with acidic humour, accompanied by a simple eyebrow-raise that was enough to crack most of her visitors up, enough to get them to stop crying and look up at her, bashfully smiling.

Charles, on the other hand, a little older than the rest of the crew, a little salt at his temples, had a charismatic earnestness that Maddie, and she suspected a few of the others, immediately identified as false. She was not *against* him; Charles had his functions, as a good diplomat and PR man. He papered over disputes, got hands shaken, made a solid impression on up-top. Still, Maddie couldn't quite find the reserves of kindness in herself to take him comfortably as he was. She found herself disagreeing with him just to disagree with him, and therefore rationed the time she had to spend with him, in groups or alone, so as not to waste the energy. And she was the one who managed the psychology reports, something Charles would never have deigned to open, preferring the personal approach, the facts of a life memorised and pulled out at just the right moment to convince another that he really had cared to know them, remember that sister who had died in childhood, the father whose absence still tore at the heart.

Still, apart from this and the other small disturbances between people in close proximity, the mood between everyone was generally peaceable. Everyone coped with the isolation and the intensity of the close confines in their own way, but together it was always this: a sequence of jokes to shift a little the structure of their days, and whenever that failed, a setting down of a layer of alcohol, for those off-shift, deep enough to drown that one common gnawing sorrow they all, for the most part, told themselves was boredom.

The morning after drinking was like all mornings after drinking on the base. Everyone got up, or, having failed to go to bed, washed their faces and moved to their task stations, or lingered over coffee and positioned themselves to make the usual comments. There is nothing like the phrase 'I'm hungover' for securing one's sense of physicality in the world. The afternoon ticked on. Then it was time for the meeting, and – nothing. No relay came through. No answer to transmission. The internet, which had been working fine up until that point, had died overnight, and nothing in Etan's toolkit, including multiple routers and brand-new cables and programs and his near endless resolute reserves of patience, would ever fix it again.

That night, the crew were only slightly unsettled by the broken link to the outside world. Charles let everyone know how this had happened once before, he'd heard, in the early days when they were testing things sans crew. Just some horrible crash of all the systems, both up-top and here. Electrical storm, or something like that. A few people nodded their heads. Maddie wondered why only Charles had heard this story. The likeliest explanation though was a malfunction. It would be fixed in a few hours at most. Or there would be some manual solution. So they got into the drinks again, with those who had been on-shift switching with those who had partied the night before. Beaumont tried out a new poem, to which people clicked their fingers, some out of play, others a little shade of cruelty. But Beaumont, as ever, didn't care. The night ended in poker, so it didn't end at all. And in the morning, the routine of work resumed as usual.

There was a five-year plan to proceedings, useful to remember in situations of more intense stress, and only, much later, towards the end, as a lightly-deluded antidote to the despair. How the first two years had gone just as could be expected, with stings of pettiness and irritability, and how the crew quickly come to function together like well-oiled cogs or a colony of ants or similarly inhuman mechanisms. They had of course passed with brilliance all required tests both on the surface interviews and pre-mission, and they had of course bonded in training and in later days over the usual things people bond over, from the broad to the specific. They had come to terms calmly but without denial with the inherent risks of the project, and the unknowability of all that could go wrong. So they were neither ants nor gears. Perhaps there was a tinge of fatalism to the general outlook, but nothing worse than that. Professionalism and the shared, self-enforced belief that they in their actions were adding to the stock of human knowledge were motivation enough to carry forwards. There were no baleful monsters at the bottom of the ocean, at least none that could get in, no night terrors beyond the dimensions of their own beds. None of them were, in the depths, incompetent – how could they be? – nor, let's say, actively bad people, even right up to the end, when the course had spun so far off the intended direction that nothing short of final orders could right it.

A week went by, and the internet would not be brought back online. Dorothy-Ann in downtime between her quartermaster work attempted to navigate the spare ROV up to the surface, "just to make contact," and was widely thought to be overre- acting. Trenton took to pestering her in the canteen by running his remote controlled car repeatedly in to the leg of her chair. At nights, with no internet to keep them distracted, the crew fell into pairing up to watch one of the three DVD films (*The Remains of the Day*, *George of the Jungle*, *Alien: Covenant*) that had inexplicably made the journey to the depths of the ocean. Or else they went off and sat alone, reading. Gossip, by that time in the run of the project, had a stale taste, like water left out. It was still a necessary part of life down here, but it didn't feel good to return to it.

After the third month without contact or supply drops, and with no way to forward on reports, work began to get lax. Some kept going at their usual diligence; the mice were kept from starvation, the 4.2 batch of low-solar seeds were germinated and divided, the cell cultures were maintained. And tending and measuring, in contrast to the drift of anxious days, was a kind of rest. Dorothy-Ann began to hold services in the chapel, mostly to an audience of Adam, Trenton and Etan. It was her line, to Maddie's ears alone, that up-top had suffered some major event, and that was why there had been no word of repairs, no shuttle. Maddie's argument against this way of thinking was that part of the experiment was to keep them all sealed up, no matter what. To thoroughly maintain integrity, visits by a crew from the surface, even if deemed below as necessary, were not permitted. The other, related argument was that this – absence of internet, slowing down of supply rations – was part of a designated test that perhaps she and Dorothy-Ann didn't have clearance to know. Both options lent Dorothy-Ann's suggestion of using the bathysphere to get up top, to seek aid, an air of traitorousness. No one should want to derail the project if this was all, in fact, part of the programme. When this idea began to circulate around some other members of the crew, Maddie had these arguments prepared, and every person eventually admitted that she was probably in the right.

Maddie took to shutting herself in her office with the sign on her door slid over to red, meaning occupied by a patient, though the only thing she was doing was working on her files. She had kept and regularly updated files on all crew members, including herself, since she had been in training with them. Necessarily at first, the data had been scanty – she had not allowed herself too much leeway in supposition. Knowledge of another's mind emerges over time, with full complex patterns of behaviour prone to shifting and evolving, so that for some people it can be easy to presume one set of behaviours observed predicts a pattern that will be somewhat lasting – but how one person might act for weeks, or even months at a time, in all kinds of circumstances provided insufficient clues, in Maddie's mind, as to how they might act on one particular day under a particular set of pressures, excitements, or after a trauma – or, even, without any evident stressors at all. She saw it in this way; that freak, shipscuttling waves are more common than we think and their causes are often inexplicable. In addition to providing the mandated counselling sessions to the crew, she had set herself the task of watching out for the freak waves, through an unorthodox method that used skilled observation, her own stream-of-consciousness writing and meditative repetition. Through this technique, Maddie thought, she was able to produce intuitive but rigorous character studies.

She would sit safe behind her occupied sign on the small grey patient's sofa and drink cup after cup of green tea made with her personal kettle, making notes on her netbook on the crew member of the day. She cycled through each of them, all eleven. Though Beaumont would have made the case to include Kaspar, Maddie was not convinced he was sufficient to qualify for personhood. She was not an expert in that particular field of study, though the question did interest her. She had studied plenty of mainstream theories of the self in her day, but what remained most true to her was that there wasn't much to it, even in actual people; that it consisted, she imagined, of a frail core, an insubstantial nub of light trembling in a net in the constant flow of external information. She pictured the meat of the self as something like a heart pierced on all sides and dissolving from the piercing, that was what everyone living was, even herself. A heart such as that could crumple under the pressure or warp to a violent shape all without visible evidence by which to notice. Maddie would notice.

Maddie limited her notes to the human crew, trying to find out their secret and flickering centres via one section on each file labelled and devoted to 'constants'. 'Constants', a single A4 page-sized part of the document, encased in a single box table, was the space in which she would write up her impression of the character and strains of the individual in question, taking her time, choosing her words carefully, then once she felt like she had written all that she wanted to, with equal care, she would delete all that filled that particular 'constants', starting from the bottom and working up, erasing each character with a jab of the backspace key, until 'constants' was emptied out entirely, returned to zero. Often she wrote the same things she had written over many previous iterations of this, her practice. What she remembered clearly enough to write down about an individual was what had been a constant in their character, or at least, enough of a constant to impress upon her over and over again in the course of her meetings and interactions with them. Sometimes she would put something new in, to give her something to work over into a 'constant', though she didn't mind if the new piece of insight proved not to be a lasting one. It gave her a calm feeling, like she was succeeding in her work as much as could be expected, and also keeping herself mentally acute, observant. In later months, as the base wound down and the crew began to die off, it gave her something to fill her time. Latterly she was tempted to stop deleting her entries, to have something that would remain behind, after they were gone. But this notion, as many times as she might hear it in her head, was a sign of weakness, a giving way to the possibility of her own mortality and the fear of the blankness that would be left behind. Which was, she thought, an utterly ridiculous and vain fear.

Maddie was working on Etan's 'constants' before he was due to come in for a check-up session prearranged over breakfast. Though each 'constants' was identical – that plain, large white square within black lines of equal indentation from the sides of the page – she thought of them as being differently coloured, depending on the day and her impressions. Today, Etan's 'constants' was a charcoal black. This was the colour she most envisioned for her own 'constants', a little like a completely dark, damp room, as in a basement, full of that black that we cannot see properly, so that looking at it makes it appear to us more a velvet-black, as our eyes struggle to process the space we are beholding. This absent-colour she understood to be the trouble we have to understand our self and how far back we sometimes stand from that pierced, flickering heart so that it does not hurt or overwhelm us to perceive it, and perceive it as dark instead. So she was surprised to see the persistent image of a dark room coming to mind over *his* space. She began writing, using a mix of old and new 'constants' in her report. As usual, upon finishing, she deleted the whole thing as usual from the bottom up. Just as she was done, Etan knocked on her office door. Maddie arranged herself behind the desk. Etan came in, a little apologetic, and sat not where she had sat, but on the black visitor's chair, leaning forward. She had noticed he always liked to let his arms sit properly on the arm rests, but it gave him an infantile look, like a young prince who has ascended to the throne before he knows what power means but knows he must look grave. After a little filler chat, he glanced over at her, then looked away.

"I miss my mom," he said, looking anywhere but in her direction. He rubbed the side of his face.

"Your mother's been dead since you were ten," she answered. "She doesn't even know you're down here."

"Sorry, yes. I – miss her grave," he said. "I think. The idea of it, what it looks like."

"No one was sending you snapchats of her gravesite, Etan." Maddie noticed with satisfaction a little piece of fluff, unassuming grey, lodged in Etan's hair. She leaned over and removed it, held it up for inspection with a serious, joking expression on her face.

"Oops," he said, with a little dry laugh, then a pause. "Yeah, thanks. You're so right, yeah. Thanks Maddie. Sorry. I'm going to try to fix the relay again, by the way." And smiled, and rose, and slunk away, leaving her door open behind him.

Dorothy-Ann set aside the missal she was holding. "We just sing psalms, talk a bit. I ask them to go back to the rites they knew as children and to lead us in the shorter prayers they know from memory. Forming the words even if they don't have faith. I think it helps," she said. "I think."

This was one Sunday afternoon in the smoky confines of the chapel nave, while everyone else was at lunch. Five months, give or take, since the last supply drop. Dorothy-Ann sat in a pew, Maddie sat on the floor. They passed the joint between them.

Strictly against the official rules, but not the rules of self-care, as both women agreed. Dorothy-Ann had let certain strictures that had once confined her good times slip. Dorothy-Ann didn't believe in a cruel God. She said she didn't believe in much but helping people hold themselves together, quietly. A false back-lit stained glass window provided the perfect setting for an encounter with the magnitude of existence, though if you really wanted to be awed, in the good, old-fashioned, terror-stricken way, all you really had to do was look out any of the front-facing windows and really focus on what you were seeing, and what you were not.

"Adam's falling to pieces, by the way. You can't tell easily, but I do think this is all getting to him, the – silence," Dorothy-Ann said.

Actually, Maddie had been trying to broach the subject for a while. Adam had grown increasingly withdrawn, even surly at times. But it was natural, and everyone went through cycles of feelings, to a greater or lesser extent, helpless in the tide of an at least outwardly unacknowledged calamity. She had not used the word calamity aloud.

"I haven't even told him what I found out," Dorothy-Ann said, gasping in and shaking out the smoke through her teeth. "That there's...nothing."

"There's usually nothing though," said Maddie. "it's the middle of the ocean."

"Directly above us, yes, but not – look. This is the thing: I navigated the ROV right to the coast–"

"Christ, that must have taken you forever. The ROV just pootles along."

Dorothy-Ann laughed and shook her head again. "It did. Ten knots, going full out. And then there are the waves, knocking it back. It took me – three bloody months it took me. I got it chugging right along there, the coast of Guam. And do you know, there were no boats. It is a little hard to see the shore, much of it anyway. But I did, I managed it. I saw the shore and everything along it. And…at night there were no lights."

"I'm sure the cam was shaking all over the place. It says nothing about what is or isn't up there. It could all be working fine. You couldn't see for shit."

"No, but that's it – I should have at least been able to see lights. But I went right round the whole island. Everything was dark. No passing ships either. It's all out. The coast is dark. It could be just Guam, but not one ship?" She blew out again, and waved her hand through the smoke to cut it and to pass the joint again.

Maddie sat quietly for a while, inhaling and blowing out through her nose. She hummed a little tune. Above them, the metal and plastic-panelled roof, and above that, black unlit weight of the ocean, and finally a thin membrane, and into the air. And in circumference around them, up there, absence. According to Dorothy-Ann. Did Maddie believe it, too? That something was missing, up where the sky and the dry world in all their fantastical colours began?

"I say we don't let them know. Don't mention it to the others. Just so as not to spread panic," Maddie said at last, "It could be an unclear picture, an incomplete picture, as much as it seems to be obvious to you what you saw. The array of saints you have at your disposal," she said, pointing hazily at the candles lit for St Francis and his pal Joseph of Aramathea, and to Joan of Arc, a framed Pre-Raphaelite girl in armour, "they will keep some of us together. Or whatever faith they have will, in God or themselves. A little delusion is a good thing. Sorry. As will the songs we sing to ourselves when we're alone, that sort of thing…"

"Sometimes you let yourself slip a little, Maddie. I like to see it," said Dorothy-Ann. She raised her head, red-eyed and smiling the way a trapped person will smile. "We'll be quiet together. We'll let them sing hymns or whatever is a comfort. We'll see it out, then."

After a pause Dorothy-Ann laughed again.

"Oh, and 'You couldn't see for shit', eh? You did sound so American when you said that."

"Yeah, dude," said Maddie, stubbing the joint out.

The days shuffled on, as much as they could be made to. Morale held steady, intermittently moderate or even good. Maddie and Dorothy-Ann kept the suspicious absence of lights along the coast of Guam to themselves. The backup ROV was returned to daily ocean-floor scanning, and it found nothing new, but each old thing was noted again, each friendly old rocky protrusion, each writhing brittle sea star catalogued a dozen times before. The crew continued to be as they were able and had been chosen to be – smart and capable and good under pressure. There was Charles to tell them what to do and how to behave while doing it, and there was Maddie to listen to their quiet moments of angst and divert them away from a downward trajectory. Everyone participated; plenty to do be getting on with all day long for the basic running of the project and upkeep of living quarters. Nightly poker games became an institution that gave free space to vent frustrations and even scores. The cigarettes no one was supposed to have, or have ever smoked, came out of their hiding places to be savoured. But there was no economy around this scant resource; that was reserved for the new crop Charles had set up.

As part of this cultivation, all of the lettuce and peas had been ripped up and made into a much-lauded salad. The only bit of truly fresh produce the crew had enjoyed for months. If Maddie could have pointed to the moment where things really started to slip, it was right there. In the salad bowl, with the oil and vinegar dressing and defrosted tomatoes grilled up, that was where the genetic future of the experimental, low-solar peas and lettuce was obliterated. She said nothing to the loss, which was, more than to anyone else on the crew, a personal loss to her, the only vegan. Even the seeds had been tipped down the sink to 'make room', or, Maddie thought, for the spectacle of Charles disposing of them, to chants of 'go, go, go' by Edward and Johnny – no more tedious, unheeded accounts of growth ratios or yield. Nothing was left of the old experiments, nothing was saved over for another generation. But there *was* weed: soon copious, self-renewing quantities of the fine green stuff, as Trenton put it, mostly processed in batches into a pan of warm oil to infuse. The vapours from the oil had nowhere to go and thickened above the stove, so that making porridge in the mornings for weeks after, Maddie could smell it, suggestive of specific nights, specific wandering hours, which she no longer wanted this much raw access to.

During one of her private sessions in her office, Maddie, working on Charles' 'constants', found herself deleting and rewriting parts of it multiple times. She found that non-clinical terms kept creeping into her notes, in particular the word *chaos*. She could find no other to replace it, even as the sentiment appeared absurd. In the end it did not matter. These were impressions only, private, for her own enlightenment on the workings of each particular mind. She deleted the entire 'constants' in the usual way, thinking dimly that her writing had not entirely fit the constraints of the practice, but that it was forgivable. She was distraught at, perhaps forever, until the end of her life, having lost access to fresh peas and lettuce. Others might be too, she thought. And now that she had written and deleted everything, she found the tension she had been holding in her shoulders begin to fall away.

Charles was clever, like everyone else in the crew, and the worst that could be said of him then was that his self-confidence had, for a second, made him sloppy, and that this confidence had at the same time obscured his sloppiness from the notice of the others, as often happens. For Maddie, she told herself it wasn't this matter of him being a slick confidence man for whose tricks people had predictably fallen, but that he should have known himself not to have done it, that something taken completely cannot be got or given back. That now the only hope for fresh produce was if the soil could make it again, say from a single missed seed, a fine, stubborn leftover of root. And that sort of miracle only happened in the grace of the surface, where there was sun and wind and a system that refuses to be entirely closed. At the bottom of the ocean is not a good place to make mistakes. Adam, the botanist, would have stepped in – there was a spare set of first-gen seeds locked in his bunk drawer, which he later revealed upon the moment he ripped open and ate them, including great quantities of other backup seeds poisonous to consumption – but at that time, when the weed was being laid in, Adam had lost the use of his words and lay most of the time in his bunk, eyes rimmed, and no one else had known at that time the secret bounty of locked drawers. This was evidence for there being levels of clearance on the base – a topic sometimes discussed, that there were parts of the mechanism of the project concealed to various ends, certain resources guarded in sealed documents or secret nooks that might have gone untapped. It was enough to get someone paranoid, even if drugs were not involved.

Charles got a second and a third crop out of the weed before his shame got the better of him. Then, as he later put it to Maddie, in passing at the dinner table, with a laugh, his wish for the weed overruled that. And no one objected, especially by that point, when obliterative levels of any drug had proved welcome, perhaps even necessary for the continued pseudo-functioning of the base.

Adam was the first one to go the chapel, at the beginning of the eighth month. It wasn't unexpected at all. In fact, most of the crew told Maddie in secret that they had thought it was long overdue that one of them would do themselves in. Some of them speculated with her who might be next. Maddie refrained from vocalising judgement – only that eyebrow, raised – but she did have to smile to herself at some of their guesses, and the various undercurrents running through their reasoning. Edward, Johnny and Ben wrapped Adam up in his bedsheet and took him to the chapel. The chiller, at that point still packed with food, had been ruled out by the squeamish, and it was cold enough in the house of God with the thermostat set right down. A crew meeting was called and the options debated. There was protocol for deaths, but these involved the outside world offering a hand. Maddie was on the side of jettisoning Adam out into the ocean, but Dorothy-Ann couldn't stand the idea of him floating out there, rotting and nibbled on by skittering hadal and abyssal creatures. She kept saying how she hated it, the idea of him floating out there, pulped and rotting and nibbled on... Eloise took her away to her bunk to sleep in the arms of a sedative. And that was how she slept from then on.

The crew discussed breaking with the mission directives altogether and heading to the surface. Burying Adam on dry land wasn't a good enough reason on its own, but the silence had been total for long enough that even the most ardent of the show-must-go-on crowd were starting to waver. So a vote was held, and the crew decided that the next day Ben and Edward would load the bathy, navigate it up to shore, hand Adam over to the authorities, and discuss things with up top to see how the project should continue. Leaving was no easy matter, freighted as it was with the admission of failure, and the possibility that neither man would be permitted to return even to inform the crew that they would have to leave. The image of the base sitting empty and useless after all that time – years of their lives – and money (other people's so it mattered less) had been shoved into its establishment was galling. Edward, though, said it was the right thing to do. He argued persuasively about the cost of set-up prohibiting an easy discard of the project. He and Ben affirmed their willingness to go and never come back, if that's what it would take. After the discussion drew to a close, Maddie went to her office, saved the file on Adam to an external hard drive and deleted the original, and emptied out the recycle bin, then sat with a cup of tea, feeling very little. Adam's 'constants' had always been some of the least interesting ones to write, since they had changed so little over time and she had never found much there, at the centre of the man. She felt she had done him justice enough with them – she had not predicted his suicide, certainly, but she hadn't exactly seen his way through safe to whatever the end would be to all this.

The next morning, before the bathy was due to depart, Maddie watched from the common room windows as a snailfish loped up from the seabed and slithered across her view. The pressure outside that window, where the tongue-coloured, tongue-shaped creature lived, would be enough to crush her body completely. So many of the vertebrates here looked like diseased organs, she thought. But what was the point of thinking that sort of thing? It would do nothing but throw off her day. She joined the others at seven am sharp for Adam's send off. Edward, Johnny, Eloise and Ben rounded the corridor bearing on their shoulders the shrouded corpse. The rest of the crew lined the walls, heads down. At the end of the corridor was the airlock. On the other side of the airlock, the bathy, readied in positon the night before. The bathy which was, on inspection, now inexplicably missing. Dark water swirled where the machine had been docked.

Who was gone? The crew looked each other over. A headcount: Dorothy-Ann was noted as missing. No, she was still sedated. Fine. Then, who had taken it? It was a mystery that could not be solved. Every single member of the crew was accounted for. Someone could have gone into the bathy, set the controls, returned through the airlock and launched it remotely from the dryside using the keycode, but that was an inexplicable amount of effort, the motive, too, seemed beyond comprehension. In lieu of trying, in lieu of accusations and rancour, Charles dismissed the mourners with assurances that the mystery would be solved in time, though it would not. The crew resumed their work for the day as best they could. Adam lay silent in the chapel, waiting on a new solution, unable to contribute his own suggestions as to what had happened to the bathysphere. It was their only way to the surface without the mission sending a second down to them, and that couldn't happen without contact resuming.

"It was Adam," said Etan with solemnity. Johnny made a dismissive noise. Someone pulled their chair back; a sharp, grinding sound.

"Just deal," Charles said, into his beer.

"Explain for us what you mean," said Maddie, who was sitting on one of the common room's other tables, holding a cup of vegetable broth in both hands, spectating on the men playing poker. It was closer to dawn than to midnight, not that anyone could tell under the LED lights. Maddie felt herself a necessary observer on what might transpire during this late session, in the wake of bathy's mysterious vanishing, the first death of the crew.

"Adam's – spirit. It, he – left," Etan said, lifting his shoulders and dropping them. Maddie looked at him sharply.

"Where did you get that idea?"

Etan shrugged, "I just think it's how it happened."

"You mean to say, Adam's ghost got into the bathy, disengaged it from the landing, and drove off with it? Adam's ghost?" said Charles.

"Uh, I don't think we can discount the weird," said Etan. "Given where we are. No one else in the history of humanity has lived down here like we have. Sorry but who knows what that does to a soul, when that soul can't get out to the light, or whatever." He addressed Charles with a kind of ardour, looking right at him until the other man was forced to blink, and finally shake his head.

"Oh man. You need to get more sleep, Etan, shit," Charles said, flicking through his cards, stubby-fingered. "It's been tough on us all but you've got your responsibilities to think of."

"Responsibilities? What ones matter now?"

"Etan, dude, you have got to keep it together. Primarily, in the first instance, don't let us down by going gaga. Funny as it might be to watch. We need you, man." He took a drink, then raised his voice. "Or you know what? Prove it to us. Just do that. I'll be big enough to admit when I'm wrong."

Maddie looked at Charles, as Charles looked at his fist around his glass. His face tilted downwards seemed a sudden mess of triangular shadows and light blown out harsh on his skin. Maddie sat up, aware of Kaspar, running between kitchen and tables on drinks duty, in his bland appealing perfection and dubious selfhood, he had nothing on Charles. Charles and his crowsfeet, and black, retreating eyes with all that lay puddling behind them. Maddie wanted, almost aggressively then, to know him; she could make an account over and over again of what she perceived as his 'constants', and had, without ever pinning what actually made this man, repugnant, charming Charles, keep going, keep smiling sardonically and upright and brisk, on days like today, on exhausting nights like this one, him sweat-stained, pallid but utterly confident in his own solidity, with the cold outside the base endlessly dark, and no one to miss them, or hear their cries should any of them be brave enough to cry out, to admit that they knew where they were in all the world down there in the depths, held back from crushing and drowning on the blood fizzling in their lungs from the pressure by a frame of metal and a penurious measure of recycled air.

"You want him to prove that life after death is a real phenomenon?" Maddie said, smoothly. "Come on now junior. Don't be foolish." Edward raised his drink and shook his head at it. Trenton laughed, once, hoarse. Maddie didn't have time to see how Etan responded, some movement too slight to catch, she guessed.

Charles smiled and gently placed his bet down on the table, with a click.

Towards 5am, Edward won the last game with a flush of clubs. Maddie postponed her 'constants' on Charles for an indefinite period. It was not a productive use of her time.

Adam remained in the chapel, a frozen slab pathetically tucked up in his white bedsheet. He swiftly found company; Johnny checked out, rather unexpectedly, slipping from this world to the next with the aid of a plastic bag and some rubber bands. Soon after, Ben fell from his bunk and split his head open against the metal desk in his room. A strange fate, given the desk had smooth, moulded edges designed to protect against the shock of a bad slip. But this was the verdict the crew decided on, an accident, abetted by drink. Ben had no enemies, after all, unless there was someone who had deeply objected to his genial wastedness in recent months or his lifelong propensity to dance to tunes of his own design, and clap his hands whenever to show his readiness.

Shortly after Ben's death, Kaspar took over the full cadre of cleaning duties. This could only be a good and necessary thing since scuffles and arguments had begun breaking out over living conditions in shared spaces. The common room had acquired an odour, present when more than one crew member had installed themselves on the lounge chairs, that many were willing to comment on and none do much about, such as to wash themselves more frequently. As if it were a sign of weakness to try to keep semblances of order over such a basic thing as basic bodily hygiene, and perhaps by then it was.

Kaspar's alacrity contrasted with this attitude of general malaise. And while he walked around performing his duties with precision, these performances were made to look like effort, even mild incompetence, to avoid offending anyone or making them jealous. He wore a selection of baseball caps picked out for him by Beaumont as the mood dictated. On Saturdays, he wore a woollen hat with a 'K' on it. After Trenton killed himself, Beaumont taught Kaspar to play poker to stop the table looking too empty. Charles objected, though the others seemed to perk up at the novelty, and Kaspar soon proved his value to the game by having the perfect face for bluffing.

Maddie, despite her intent to pay him less attention began to notice that something had turned in Charles. He talked rougher and faster, he leaned on the backs of people's chairs when they were sitting on them. He also, she saw, seemed to be avoiding the windows as much as he could manage, and as smoothly as he could. He spent a lot of time in the kitchen at the counters that faced the wall, doing whatever meal-based task needed to be done – he was a good cook, Charles, if a carnivore – while using his time there to keep a glancing but hard eye on the events of the common room as they unfolded without him. Whether the others noticed this uptick in intensity or not varied; some did, and chose to keep out of his way, others interacted in the usual friendly manner, with only little glimmers of doubt visible on their faces as Charles took another turn about the room or stood too close as they were talking. Dorothy-Ann was the sole person whose mood towards him improved. They shared the bio shift, tending to living conditions of the mice, though no longer testing or selecting them for breeding.

Dorothy-Ann sat with Charles more and more often, letting him rest his hand on her shoulder, offering to take his plate up after meals. Whispering low together, more than a few times, in the corridors, glancing about as if in conspiracy. Charles' sudden harsh laughter came more often. Maddie felt herself harden still further. She waited for Charles, inevitably to break. It would be, she reasoned, a fairly typical outburst of aggression. She would know what to do when it happened, how to talk him down, de-escalate the others, how to rehabilitate him after the crisis was passed.

The common rooms, aside from their pernicious stink which nothing would banish, once again looked clean and orderly thanks to Kaspar. Eloise began to pay him more attention, and it made a strange sight to see her, tall and big-armed, drifting beside him as he worked through the base, talking as he cleaned, keeping up a lengthy monologue on her previous life and current opinions while he made the appropriate noises and occasionally shook his head. One afternoon Eloise sat in the common room while Kaspar scrubbed away the base inhabitants' messes, their skin cells and discharges, from the floor and walls. She kept up her speechifying, this time, on a memory she had as a young girl walking under some flowering trees – she couldn't remember which sort, and was trying over and over to describe the look of the tree, the shape of the florets, and their perfume in the spring air. Maddie was watching *George of the Jungle* with Etan and Edward, all three uninterested in the noise from Eloise, and in any case the subtitles were on, helping the cries of jungle animals into the coherence of human letters. Edward occasionally joining in with his interpretation.

"Elephant trumpets!" he read. He leapt to his feet, motioned playing a tune in Etan's direction.

"That's a saxophone! A trumpet's like this," Etan said, making his own hand gestures and puffing out his face.

"Oh no, I know. Elephants would totally play sax," Edward replied. Maddie was just about to wave them both down, when

Charles walked into the room, poured himself a coffee, and sat brooding, turned away as ever now from the windows that faced the trench.

"When are you going to shut up?" he said to her at last. "That tinpot doesn't care. We don't care. You're taking up valuable oxygen letting your mouth run hot garbage."

Eloise said nothing. Then she looked about her, as if she had remembered something, and suddenly ran from the room. Maddie sat looking calm, as she had to. The oxygen around them was unwasteable, constantly renewed by a self-sustaining system, even if the occupants of the base were not. After a moment, Charles got up and left too. Maddie waited. Kaspar resumed his work, moving on to buffing the mould out of the kitchen backsplash. No one else but Maddie, Etan and Edward appeared to be around, but that was getting to be more and more the case during the day as people took to napping away the hours, throwing themselves down deeper than the depths they were already in by any and all chemical means. At some point Beaumont walked in and gave a nod to Etan and they went to the chess board, carefully rearranging the pieces. Edward turned off the jungle and began reading a book he had borrowed from Johnny when Johnny was still alive. It looked like the kind of book Johnny and Edward would both like; it had a battleship on the cover, dramatically bursting through deep swells.

Maddie imagined all of them in that room as players in a silent movie. In the standard black uniform and black beanie hats the figures sat against a grey backdrop on their off-white chairs. Only the red wristband of Etan's watch broke into her vision now and then, as he darted his hand around the board. Edward left. Etan won the game and also disappeared. Beaumont pulled out a notebook and began writing. After an hour, Eloise returned. She sat on the sofa by the window and picked up a magazine. She had a bruise under her eye and her breathing was barely controlled. Kaspar had finished the grouting, wiped down the counters and disposed of the rubbish. No one spoke.

He came back, stood a moment lost in the doorway, before he walked up to Beaumont and smiled.

"You can take a break now," said Beaumont softly. Maddie noticed Beaumont carefully not looking at Eloise, but finding her in the room anyway. Eloise was intent on the page about the stars of a film which had come and gone from cinemas ten months previously, and which she could not in any case watch given the internet remained inaccessible. Maddie wondered about the way she caressed the edge of the lead actress' dress, a complex dark colour with touches of light on it in gold; the night sky in a baroque painting.

"Take a break for the evening, Kaspar. Go recharge, there's a good kid," Beaumont said, pausing a moment, picking up a cup and looking around. The kitchen gleamed, a dab of blue on the floor where Kaspar had tried and failed to hang up the dish towels – one of his gestures towards incompetence, there to show that he was not better than anyone else just because he could do it better. The chairs of the common room sat empty, aside from the two still, seated women.

"Poker tonight?" said Maddie.

"You want to play?" Beaumont said.

Maddie nodded.

"Wagers are getting high up there," said Beaumont, putting the notebook away in a pocket. "I don't go for it. I'm having an early night. You'll have to put up something big just to get in."

"Don't you worry about that," Maddie said, looking over at Eloise, feeling her throat constrict. "I'll bring something to the table."

As Maddie wrote in Beaumont's 'constants' that afternoon she reflected as usual that they had been at first a bit of a mystery, in that they seemed to have no deep neuroses to uncover, and therefore seemed to be an example of project HR having rare success in hiring just the right sort of person for a job like this: a completely straightforward person, a slightly cool, competent, professional individual who merely wants to do their job well. This character profile was common in aeronautics, but subaqua research was a quixotic field and attracted people quicker to laughter and eccentricity. She felt, even as she wrote on them with detachment, that Beaumont was, being honest, a boring fixture. Even the poems Beaumont wrote were very reasonable and pleasant. She shook her head, remembering the times when Beaumont had some insightful thing to say when the moment called for it, or how they kept quiet if there was nothing to be said. They reminded her of a character from a children's book, someone wise and mysterious who came and went on their own, refused to get involved in the great battles or intrigues, and usually smoked a pipe of some kind. Maddie knew that if she had it in herself to be Beaumont, she would, if she could stand to find out the truth of how little there was to the skill of being them.

Charles was screaming: Maddie heard him at it as she was approaching the store. It had been three days over a year since the last supply drop. She peered round the corner and ducked as blind with anger Charles threw an archival box at the corridor, where it popped open and, as if in afterthought, spread out the list of inventory slips at her feet. He came to the doorway, looked at her with fury, and then left. In the store packets lay strewn everywhere, torn open, unreconstituted dust and noodles broken by a heel. Tins had been kicked about, oozing meat where the sides had split under the force of a hammer, which lay covered in muck inside one of the glass refrigerators, door now shattered and hanging off its hinges. One of the store's metal chairs with the back ripped off choked a high shelf, its battered legs sticking out at angles. Several weights from the gym had been thrown at the freezers, and the freezers unplugged long enough that standing water had begun to crawl up to every wall. In the mess stood Etan and Edward, looking at Maddie. The light fixtures had been ripped down, but were still working, casting Etan and Edward in eerie light as they bent and began picking through the goods, trying to see what could be salvaged. Maddie watched them a while. From Dorothy-Ann's room upbeat pop music was blaring. No one had heard anything before Charles' tantrum.

"Do you think it was her?" Etan asked.

Maddie said, "Are you sure it wasn't Charles?"

"Charles came and got us," said Edward. "No way. Did you see him? He's furious."

"Well. I can't account for Dorothy-Ann. Perhaps, perhaps in a fugue state, maybe. But otherwise I can't see her doing this much damage."

"Eloise was missing for an hour, right?" said Edward, but Etan raised his hand to Edward's arm and shook his head. "No, man. I know where she was," he looked meaningfully down the corridor to where Charles had gone.

Maddie gave him a questioning look, but Etan avoided her eye and continued to examine the spoil.

Eloise had been otherwise occupied. That bruise on her face. Charles. Maddie knew she should investigate it further, but she was – she admitted to herself only much later – at that time still afraid of the idea of an open sortie with Charles, knowing that he could so easily swing the mood of the crew against her. She filed her suspicions away in a dimly lit place – thinking she would broach something at the poker that night. She was alone in this, she knew. Everyone was trying their hardest to quietly continue in a steady direction. And they were right to do so, until they were wrong to do so, wilfully ignoring suffering, hiding themselves from the truth. Complicit, she thought. But for herself she allowed leeway, until later, when she had steeled herself and knew what was best to do.

As to who was responsible for the trashing of the store, it seemed to be beyond Dorothy-Ann's strength, but you never knew, Maddie thought. You never knew what someone was capable of. Even if you had trained for years to know it, had grown intimate little whiskers for sensing that twinge of another towards the point of break. Maddie mutely fetched some plastic tubs, the kind used to transport clothing to the base, and began scooping and cracking out what she could from the ruined tins. Savoury into one tub, sweet in another. Against the wall, the only things left almost untouched stood in a row – the plastic twenty-gallon bins of powdered milk in different flavours, lids ripped off but too heavy for the assailant to get them tipped over, or perhaps something else had stayed their hand. Some of the men had a childish obsession with strawberry milk, salted caramel flavoured milk, saying more than once that the taste reminded them of drinks from their schooldays, or something they had had as a treat, their mothers in the kitchens of their youth, some rainy after-school afternoon, making them up this artificial, sugar-pumped bovine-origin gift and handing it to them with a smile. Maddie's own mother had refused to buy such junk. This particular powdered milk formula was protein and vitamin enriched, and some people drank it if they felt in need of a pick-me-up after working out. It sweated from their pores; it made them feel as if they were getting stronger, it comforted them as if remembered familiarity granted it a kind of intimacy to bestow, a reconstituted hug in place of real ones now forever out of reach. It made her shudder. She could feel it collecting under her nails as she scraped up salvaged food. She could taste the powder on the air and it tasted like dried body secretions, she thought. No, it didn't really. It tasted only of overwhelming sweetness; everything else, she sighed, came from her particular prejudice against it.

Down on her hands and knees Maddie began, in spite

of herself, to think about the world high above their heads, the place where the light was, the air, variable weather. She imagined walking into a restaurant, a Japanese restaurant that had once been a regular stop, and ordering a tofu hotpot and a green tea. She pictured herself far away from the dirty floor of the storeroom, sitting instead by a window, a window that faced a busy world – she saw herself watching the crowds walking by through the sleet, heads bent against the wind, small dogs walking quickly amongst them. The wooden door creaking as parties came in and out of the restaurant, blowing in swirls of cold air. She sat alone. She saw a shucked edamame bean, shining bright, held between her two chopsticks and popped in her mouth. This was her form of nostalgic desire, just as pathetic as that of the milk-drinkers, but better, she told herself, for being desire for a memory of a meal she had chosen for herself. Not for her the warmth for cheap sugary mixes bought as a bribe for a child's affection or happiness, a means of quietening them down. She imagined the rice, undersides turning golden brown from the heat of the stone pot. She remembered buying herself this meal for the first time as a student, saving up the cash and taking herself into food territories that her mother had never dreamed of trying. She remembered salt, and crispiness, and the quivering soya bite of the tofu. She had made that choice. She had chosen how best to be in the world, ethical, brave. She was her own woman, in all things.

In the store room there was about a month's worth of solid food remaining, even after recovering canned meat and peaches from the floor. To survive for a little while longer, Maddie would have to eat meat again, or she could turn it down and keep her principles and live without disgust. She would starve to death anyway sometime after that month, the same as all the rest. Maddie let her legs come out under her on the floor and canning liquids oozed under the backs of her knees, her palms. The men continued their diligence, picking up the scattered supply drop papers, talking softly now, far away. She asked herself if she might like to be high for the poker game that night. But not on weed; on whatever industrial chemicals she could round up, some truly fortifying witches brew. The game would be difficult, and every day would be difficult, and the deaths were going to continue, and she would rather not care at all, even as she chose her own way towards an ending. She licked gritty syrup from her fingers.

For a second, she almost asked Etan and Edward who they thought would turn cannibal first. But why pre-empt the bets now? There was the evening to consider.

After what had been salvaged had been salvaged and what could be put in order had been put in order, Maddie went to Dorothy-Ann's room from which music was still throbbing. The door was locked, but Maddie had months before on a slow day hacked her lanyard and could be admitted everywhere. Dorothy-Ann was lying on top of her covers in her day uniform, which was covered in food stains and rips. Her hands were in fists, her hair ratty, also full of food slop. Around her cheerful music raged. Maddie sat down on the desk, knees up, staring at the poster on the back of Dorothy-Ann's door; it was a picture of Trinity College Library, hypnotic with symmetrical rows of books.

"Oh, Dorothy-Ann," she said, shaking her head. "Why?"

"Trenton was here," Dorothy-Ann replied, almost inaudible.

Trenton had gone out peacefully, leaving a song lyric on his phone's notes and his door helpfully ajar.

"No, he wasn't" Maddie said in a consoling voice.

"No, he wasn't," said Dorothy-Ann. Her eyes were bloodshot. On her arms were long scratches. "Charles was here. Charles came here. I let him in."

"Do you want to tell me about it?" Maddie said, turning the speaker down low, keeping her voice level. "And did he say – I have to ask this, Dorothy-Ann, I think you're the one who might know – did he hurt you?

"Turn it up again! Turn it back up!"

Maddie turned it back up almost all the way, slipped off the desk and went to Dorothy-Ann, standing over her. If she knelt down it would seem too much a death-bed confessional. In any case a look was enough to stretch the terrible weight between them.

"Never mind then. Tell me something else. Did he tell you if he had some – involvement with the other's deaths? With the bathy? I think he might have. I think he thought you'd listen – but perhaps you reacted in some way he couldn't take?"

"He came to check in with me," Dorothy-Ann said blankly. "He was very calm. Pass me that makeup bag, would you?"

If Charles had let anything slip, had threatened her into wrecking the food, or gloated or howled in animal rage after she had done it, and Maddie had somehow missed the moment, Dorothy-Ann wasn't saying. She was keeping his secrets and her own motivation, and she would forever. What did it matter? Above the two women, the whole wide ocean lay thick and freezing and indifferent. You could start to think of that great presence too much even when you weren't thinking of it, even when you thought you had got over thinking of it in concrete or even abstract terms it still found a way to bear down, and the bright lights of the living quarters were too bright, and the air too dry, imagine it, so that your eyes watered in involuntary response.

Maddie flinched: Dorothy-Ann was laughing, clutching a lipstick, squeezing the soft bullet between her fingers until it distorted and fell off the plastic. Dorothy-Ann covered her mouth. Maddie removed the two pieces of the lipstick. On the desk was a vanity mirror, and she held this up to Dorothy-Ann so that the woman could see her face. She helped Dorothy-Ann tuck her food-slicked hair behind her ears and smooth out her eyebrows, and she helped Dorothy-Ann apply a dab of the lipstick from her fingertips to her cracked lips, concealer under her eyes. When that was done Maddie turned off the music, and Dorothy-Ann sighed. They sat in the new silence a while.

"I think he knows there's nothing now, up there," Dorothy-Ann said, "I think I told him, and didn't do it well. Not as gently as he needed. Here. We, you and I, we can sit with it. But he can't. We didn't give him enough time."

"We weren't going to tell him," said Maddie, "We didn't give him time because what would that have helped? Any of them?" The room was silent with the non-sounds that kept it going; the hum of the AC, the quiet washing sound of the pipes. "You know, I think. I could fight him." Maddie began, dreamily, "I could – I think I could murder him, with my bare hands. There's so much he has done, I know it. I could try to understand him. But I think I'd rather – I'd punch him in his fucking eyes. Put them right out. I could squeeze. Around his neck. I could hold him down. I could kill him."

She took a sharp breath in. Dorothy-Ann swivelled her eyes to hers.

"There isn't any benefit to talking like that," she said, slowly, "as I see it. The others will be here – it might hurt them. To hear you say it and to imagine you might do it. Even if you wanted to there isn't a single place left to fight, to move at all without bashing into someone else. It's all very small," she wriggled, her head disappeared under her blanket. "Even under here, there's no space at all. We've all swollen up with our lives and our feelings and there isn't a centimetre of space that's free." Her voice muffled, "I'm too hot."

"It's interesting to see who copes and how they go about it, and how they develop strategies that are selfish, sometimes, or try to support other people," Maddie said, sitting down beside her, "take the blanket off your head."

"I don't think I'm doing well," said Dorothy-Ann, doing as she was told.

"No," said Maddie. "You're doing remarkably well."

After a time, Dorothy-Ann said, "I always loved the sea." She looked up at the ceiling panels. "But I didn't understand it from the inside out, not before I came here. It's not how we look at it, the sea. We go from the shore out, from the shape of the waves, not imagining how it must look at the very bottom, and when we do see that, it's only in videos, ever. How funny, I've seen what the ocean looks like for so long, stared out at it in a way most other people don't ever even think of. Me! Charles is frightened by it. It makes him feel so desolate you know, no light from the surface, nothing of us this far down but us, and us with no way out. But I like it, in a way, seeing it. It's so pure out there – like having access to a wonder nobody else knows about. But, well, maybe – is it even a wonder then? You can't see the edges, you can't tell anyone. Maybe it's right that we can't anymore."

Silence again.

She took a shuddering breath. Maddie waited for Dorothy-Ann to tell her more about Charles, but she did not.

"We forget it's dark in here too," Dorothy-Ann said, patting her chest. "Did you know," she said, with a faraway look on her face, "did you know that the heart burns up in electrical fire, each time it beats. Everywhere there's light to find, even in the forgotten places. A small spiny fish, a cellular burst. Inside I feel it like my heart's getting a Viking funeral. No one can see it, but it's still happening."

Another moment of silence.

"I'm quite poetic. I didn't put that on my entrance form, but I am. I love words. Even the word ocean. It just sounds right."

Maddie said, "Where do you want to go now, Dorothy-Ann?"

"I want to go home."

"Well," said Maddie. "Home. I've got some engagements here, so I'm staying. I can't tell you what to do though." She folded her hands on her lap. Dorothy-Ann stared at her, eyes wide and deeply set, the eyes in a photograph of someone in shock. Her voice was calm.

"If you want to help me, I'd appreciate it."

"Anything. What do you need?"

"Help me up? I want to go to the chapel."

191

"Are you sure? It's pretty bad in there, even with the temperature cranked down."

"Adam's there. Trenton's there. God's there."

"Isn't God everywhere, didn't you tell me that?"

"I didn't tell you that," said Dorothy-Ann, "I think it's fine though. If it's is a sin to claim God is somewhere God is not, it's a small one. Now, now it's a small one. Other people wiser than me would be able to say, theologists, you know –" she waved her hand vaguely, "More pills in the drawer behind you. I've had quite a lot already."

Maddie helped lift her to standing and put on her shoes and a cardigan.

"Right, looking smart," Maddie said, taking out three blister packs of tablets from the small cabinet. "Is there much left in the dispensary?"

Dorothy-Ann did not respond. She grabbed her pillow and walked to few steps to the door. The poster of the library caught Dorothy-Ann's attention for just a moment. Books retreated infinitely ahead of her. "I wish I'd taken anything else than this."

The hallway was deserted. In the chapel they sat with the dead lumpen around them in white sheets, and the stained glass window illuminated their living shoulders and faces. Maddie put a song on, one of the selection that the podium apparently had available to an expected congregation of religious scientists – they might have come later, Maddie supposed. It was an easy-listening hymn without words. It filled the space with a poignant warmth that Maddie disliked, in the circumstances. She turned it up as loud as it would go. Dorothy-Ann smiled, though thinly.

"Good enough?" Dorothy-Ann asked.

"Good enough," Maddie answered.

In the shadow between the pews, Dorothy-Ann lay down. The additional pills took a long time, and did not finish her cleanly, and her eyelids flickered, and drool came out of her mouth. Maddie rose, walked over to the podium, and turned off the music. Then she walked back purposefully down the aisle and kneeled at Dorothy-Ann's side, whispering to her a while. Then Maddie put the pillow over Dorothy-Ann's face. Dorothy-Ann wouldn't have wanted to have gone out sloppily, remained an extra mouth to feed after all that she'd done. Even if it meant this, Maddie as murderer. There was no sound, no movement of resistance.

After the other body was still, Maddie sat with her numb hand on her own chest, tearless, filling the silent space with awful, pointless gasps.

That night at the poker, Edward and Etan and Kaspar and Charles and Maddie up to play. Eloise was taking an overdose of lorazepam in her room and would be discovered with Dorothy-Ann much later the next day. Edward dealt. Kaspar lost the first round almost immediately.

"Oh dear," he said, in a balanced voice.

Charles lit a joint and passed it around. Maddie sat under the layer of the drugs she had ingested, a blend that left her brave and retooled her numbness, put a fever in her skin and filled her with some other feeling whose name she could not locate, that felt like artificial sweetener dissolving in the soul. Under the influence of the drugs the room smelled almost like nothing, though the room was filled with the long unwashed. Maddie herself had not washed her hands after all that had transpired.

"What's the stakes tonight?" Charles asked.

"What do you mean?" said Etan. "The usual. Some cash. What would we play for?"

"What are we going to spend cash on?" said Charles, shaking his head. "We're never leaving here."

After that, in silence, they ran a short couple of games, betting money anyway. Sour, uninteresting things with little bluffing and lots of drink. At last Charles groaned.

"Gotta get this *going*. Let's play for something that has meaning, goddamn," said Charles.

No one said anything.

"Goddamn, I want—" said Charles.

Maddie waited. It was Etan who caved first.

"What do you want Charles?"

There was a look on Charles' face. His teeth showed. He had a shading of stubble on his face where it was normally clean-shaven, even in these, the latest of all days.

"*Pussy*," he said, rapping once on the table. Edward laughed and hooted. Maddie looked at all of them. Animals. Etan, predictably, covering his awkwardness with fumbling gestures and a shake of his head, as if to say, oh you joker, when even he knew. Kaspar stared off beyond his imperatives, at a quiet loss for what to say.

"Fine, let's play for that, then," Maddie found herself saying. A bead of sweat ran down her back into her underwear.

"I play to keep, my dear," Charles said.

"Pussy!" said Edward. Etan threw his arms at him and pushed, playfully, and not.

At this Maddie smiled, rose and went to the kitchen. She pulled a knife out of the cutlery drawer. Nothing big, just a butter knife. She brought it back to the table and held it up for inspection and placed it down on the poker table, adjusting its position until it was level on the horizontal.

"We play for parts," she said, "If Charles wins, he gets to have my pussy. To keep." She nodded at the knife. Edward drew away from the table in horror.

"What the fuck Maddie? You are not serious right now."

Etan, after a slow moment of realisation, got up and moved to where Edward was standing. He was shaking his head, he was washing his hands. Maddie showed him her teeth.

"Maddie, for fuck's sake," he said. "That's not a good joke."

Charles stood up and put his hands on the back of the chair

and looked at the knife, then, gave an almost imperceptible smile.

"Are you for real?"

She nodded.

"All right," Charles said. "And what about you, Edward?" he said, not breaking gaze with Maddie. "You want to cut out Maddie's pussy and carry it off to your bunk?"

"Ha fucking ha, man," said Edward.

"You, Etan?" Charles asked. Etan shook his head.

"Kaspar?"

"I don't know what you to say."

"No, you wouldn't, you wouldn't. So who's going to play?"

"And if I win, overall, I get to take whatever piece of you I want," Maddie said in a level voice.

"Fine," said Charles, looking at Etan, Edward and Kaspar in turn. "Let's – fucking – play."

In silence, the players sat down.

The first game went to Edward, and Etan lost all his chips. Maddie saw him play his hand for the purpose of losing, but did not comment; likely enough the rest saw how he had fumbled his way through the game without even trying to hide his exit strategies. She would not judge his actions, she told herself, and in the gaps between plays found herself studying the faint scuffed and raw patches on his unsunned, sallow skin and wonder if he had taken to scratching at it in times of stress, and why, if so, he hadn't reported this behaviour. Maybe he didn't know how bad it had become, like a dog chewing on its tail until the fur gets thin, full of misery, never knowing any better. He lost, he got up from his seat and went to the kitchen where he made himself a hot drink out of one of the milks and sat far away from the table where the rest still played. But he did not leave the room. Maddie could feel him turning his head to look, now and then, his eyes blinking more than they usually did, narrowed against the harsh lights and the lateness of the hour. She began to sweat in earnest, and enjoyed it as a counter to the cold buzz of her flesh and the occasional warping of the room. As the games progressed in mostly silence Maddie had no focus left to spare with which to wonder at each tweak she was making to her performance, or to think on what the stake truly meant, trusting instead that her impulsive gesture was to make something change, to stop something, or alter it completely before they all ran completely aground. Whether that was possible or not – she wiped her face with the back of her sleeve – she would be ready. The chips tickered together, shifted about between fingers and table. Kaspar made small noises of consideration and defeat, though Edward was the next out.

Maddie, Kaspar, Charles. Maddie looked at her hands where they held the edges of the table between turns, cards arranged between her thumbs. Streaks of light flashed brightly over the cards and her hands, writhing like lightning, like the fractal arms of a basket star, but never escaping their limit in the glossy paper and in her bones, muscles, veins, and so they remained hidden, and so nothing changed. The common room where they had all spent months of their lives at wait was still all grey, and the base with its many plain corridors leading off was grey and the rivets and smooth sectioning and bunkrooms all alike, all that same shade of grey, different to the grey space visible outside and almost as bleak. If only the light could extend even slightly from her, Maddie thought, flow out of her hands so she could give her energy, give some way for them all, here, still alive, to have a robust, vital grounding in the world. But, she thought, in others you've only ever put that light out. She blinked – a jolt of static electricity – and started back. No one at the table even noticed.

That was something that could have been discussed in one of the relays, she thought, shifting tack: circadian rhythms should have been linked better to the lighting of living quarters, get a sense of vivacity and meaning derived from right colours and you evade the grinding effect of colour limitation. Definitely, yes, if the colours and the lighting had been better managed tensions might have discharged and none of this would have happened. She was surprised she hadn't thought of it before now, before her head was a floating bubble above her body, above the knife shining on the grey tabletop and her hands electric below it. She had thought of paint changes quite early into the project, and had decided to bring it up at a meeting, but Charles had interrupted just as she was clearing her throat and said it was an issue of fumes in a confined space. He had wanted instead to talk about new avenues of sampling and exploration for the ROV, so that was what they talked about in that meeting, even though that was not Charles' area of expertise, or even interest.

"Five minute break?" asked Kaspar.

Everyone left the table. Charles went to Etan and Edward, both propped up against the counter that divided the kitchen from the common room, and stood by them, drinking, braying with laughter. Etan and Edward, unseen by Charles, gave one another a look. Maddie slid by them, into the toilets, and washed her face. In the mirror over the sink she saw that she had long dirty strands in her hair, and that one of her irises had a crack in it, a fine white crack. She touched the skin under her green eyes, she pulled out some of the dirty strands and washed them down the sink, disgusted. In her mouth her teeth felt like sunfish teeth, extending in circular rows all the way down her throat. And then she thought, that's good, it gave her the chance to take on Charles, where before she could not have managed, now she could attack him, with a chance, floor him, consume him in chunks with her mouth, tear at him the way a fish tears at a floating corpse, letting most of it tumble and waste in the space of the water, lacking the grip of claws to keep it still.

"You are too high," Maddie told herself. Perhaps her line of thinking was too vindictive towards the man. She had after all killed a woman today. The thought was bracing. The rest of the people in this room, in this base, didn't know that about her, that she was a killer, and that she felt in particular nothing about that except a little alarm. Perhaps, if she lifted up one corner of herself, something true and ugly about herself would slither away from her gaze. Well, and if so, if her behaviour and her thoughts now and earlier were not justifiable responses to outrageous conditions or close confines with flawed people in outrageous conditions, well, what of it? They *were*. She washed her face again and rubbed it in slow circles with the hand towel, until it was dry.

Maddie was in the common room again. She looked at Charles; he appeared thoughtful and calm while the other men now kept their distance, talking amongst themselves at the far side of the room over cups of sickly milk, made up hot and steaming. She felt very sure now the back corners of his brain were stuffed to overflow with mud and slime: he was angry, wrong-footed, she thought at once. Charles always looked his most reasonable when he was furious. Yes, Charles was angry, and often so, that was why she hadn't liked to spend much time with him, why she was unsuccessful in her attempts to under-stand him and his condition to the betterment of the running of the base. Under his skin was lava and animal fur and animal need. Blood moved in his shadow. He thought only of himself. Eloise's eye got blackened for her slight disruption of his façade. Dorothy-Ann came all undone, and Charles might have undone her before she destroyed all the food, he might have done something to her, and Maddie might have, for all her vigilance, let it go unwitnessed, and now Dorothy-Ann was dead. The toxicity was concealed for the most part in Charles so that only the slightest breeze, slightest hint, could waft the stench off his rage and reach her subconscious, not enough to justify a self-de-fensive, open hostility towards him, but enough to instruct her, without giving reason why, to hold herself firmly back. Maddie did not have a history with angry men, but, she told herself, she did have a strong self-preserving instinct. She had hoped others would sense the danger in Charles, not so she could feel righteous in company, but to stop her from feeling quite so alone, so that now, in the chaos – she was unafraid to use that word now – she could have known there was another person on board on her side, who would point a finger at Charles, have him locked down, confined to where he belonged, in a small, neutral space. It was the hope of civility, even in the action of the wreck.

Her skill in identifying Charles before the rest managed to, she told herself, came from a judicial survival instinct that extended itself in vegan generosity to all other creatures, though perhaps, as had been demonstrated throughout her life, not as generously as she would have wished. After all, she had never opened the gates to a slaughterhouse, she had only ever petitioned the government of her country on the matter of animal welfare via online forms requiring little more than a few clicks, and sooner or later, she was going set aside her principals and drink the awful powdered milk rather than let herself die. Briefly she thought that she had not shared her distaste for Charles with anyone else, and that perhaps this was the worst outcome of her passivity, her waiting until forced, at the absolute limit of what she would take. But inwardly she absolved herself. She alone had chosen the position of scrupulous guard on duty, staring in upright post, resisting Charles as he got himself over everyone who could not see. Because of him, she thought, against her will, threatened the end of the world, and her lostness was like calcifying dirty veins inside her, and she had no weapon, just her hands and their energy, her endurance and her judgements. All it takes is a single person to stand up and say they will not be deceived, that if they are going to be crushed, then they will not allow their dignity to be crushed too.

Maddie was breathing very fast. She was sitting at the table, cards in hand again, the room filling up with breath, the oxygenating system of the base waiting to suck that breath in until it had enough to cycle and spit back out again for a second, third, however many breaths for all remaining functional lungs. If she had to make herself unlikeable to make a stand against Charles now, at this late moment, that was fine. But you could be entirely wrong, she thought, about the whole situation, about Charles. He could be no better and no worse than you. He'd probably tell me that, she thought. I'm no worse than you, Madeleine. No more fucked, that's for sure. And then he'd smile, so evenly, and she'd believe him, she'd allow herself to believe him, and apologise. The room was filling up with oxygen-depleted breaths. Kaspar had his play in hand.

In her bunk, Eloise was dying, asleep at it, causing no fuss. Back out in the common room, Kaspar played a four of a kind. Charles swore and stood up to kick his own chair half-way across the room. On the common room sofa Etan looked in shadow, Edward too. Maddie laughed in private at lights shimmering on the floor as she stared at them, because it suddenly made it seem as if they were sitting together at the bottom of a swimming pool, and with that, as if it would be that easy to swim upwards through the clear blue water, to the surface, within a strong kick's reach. Stop thinking of it all as water, she told herself, it's air now, out there, and in here's the aberration, right? For this moment and maybe not much longer. She had her hand on her chest, making sure it was moving in and out.

"Sit down, Charles," she said. She would give nothing away, her surfaces were calm as Kaspar's were. If they were all like Kaspar, none of them would have disintegrated, died. Or been killed. She leaned over to pat Kaspar on the head, then pulled back her hand. She did not want to invade his space, and, thinking about it, it was a little odd, that kind of gesture, for her. In the game that followed, Maddie forced herself to relax. She was fine at the bluff, she knew that her sparking, shifting body was under her control. She had a winning hand, and won. And won again.

"If things were going along as usual," said Kaspar, "we might think about starting the working day." He folded shortly after. Maddie felt her head buzzing. She wondered if Kaspar was clever enough to let her win: It was possible he knew how to diffuse the situation where she had worked out only how to escalate it. Maddie rubbed her eyes, made them blurry. She felt deeply tired; she wanted to sleep for twelve years, she wanted never to get up from this table, or move her head even slightly.

Charles was looking at her.

"What are you holding, girlie?"

He had never called her that before, and he knew very well what he was doing.

"Make me tell."

"If I didn't know you for a consummate bitch of a professional ice queen I'd say you were getting ready to slap me. You got that look. But I do, so I think it's a losing hand, now," he said, slurring his words lightly. Maddie thought about how best to proceed for a moment, and settled on standing, and laying her cards, with scrupulous neatness, on the field of play.

"Royal flush," she said.

"No," said Charles, slapping his hand down, petulant. "Bullshit. Cheater."

"Don't be juvenile, Charles."

"Coming from you, Maddie," said Etan. He was slumped over on the sofa now, the black screen behind him making a definitive frame. His voice echoed. Edward stood up and helped Etan up. Charles stood too. He was a little shorter than Maddie, hardly noticeable until positioned in this way, facing her off. He also had green eyes, when the light hit them, as now. She squinted; she put one hand on the knife.

"What piece of me are you going to take then?" he said. "You going to cut off my dick? You going to take my dick back to your bunk, Maddie? Is that what you're going to take from me?"

"Your innocence," Maddie said.

"Wow. Oh wow," said Charles. "Flattered – but it's been some time since that was on the table."

"I mean in the other sense."

"The other sense of innocence? What sense is that, Maddie?"

"The kind that lives in opposition to guilt."

The words furred in her mouth as she spoke, but Charles

moved his head back very slightly. Good, thought Maddie. Now I've got you.

"The piece I want is the truth of what you did," she went on. "What you've been doing."

The knife still lay on the table under Maddie's palm. She had it up as soon as Charles flinched.

"Don't," she said, gripping the knife close.

"Don't," he said at the same time. Fear in his low voice.

They both sat down. The others in the room did not hide that they were the audience, locked in to watching. Maddie glanced at them. Etan, Edward, Kaspar. This is a serious lineup of serious men, machine and me, she thought.

"Did you kill Adam?" she asked. "Or Johnny?"

"What? No," said Charles. "That was suicide, both cases. Shit."

"Did you release the bathysphere?"

"...no."

"I don't believe you. Did you destroy the food?"

"That was Dorothy-Ann."

"Did you hurt Dorothy-Ann? Did you break her in some way, push her to madness?"

"No. Nuh-uh."

"Liar. What about Eloise?"

"What about Eloise?"

"Did you beat her? Did you do worse?"

Charles looked away. He had a grim smile on his face.

"Ask me about something else as stupid as that. Ask me about, like, walking around outside the base, twirling a baton."

"Liar. About everything that matters, you lie. Talk straight to me now. Tell me the truth. This is what I win: I win the truth from you. So pay it out. Tell me everything you did to fuck us all."

"You don't like me very much, do you Madeleine?"

"No, I do not, Charles."

"Aren't you going to ask me the most important question?"

Maddie paused. "Is any of this real?"

"You mean?"

"Is any of this situation we are in real? Did you manufacture it in some way, like cutting the wires to the surface, or rerouted them somehow, sending messages that we were fine, shutting us down, keeping us here when we could have got out – I want to know, did you have some part in a mission that we weren't to know about, that had you set all of this up?"

Some shuffling from the two men at the counter. Charles was still smiling, but the smile was fading.

"Well, did you?" asked Etan. It was ironic, and it wasn't. Maddie gripped the edge of the table again, and lowered herself to sitting, still holding the knife, and Charles stood. He kept opening his mouth, shaking his head, and when he spoke, his tone was soothing.

"Maddie, no. Inventive stuff but why in the shit would I do that? Why would CURA do that? In case you ask again no, I didn't do any of the things you seem to think I did, or could have done. I'm not a villain, I'm not the bad guy, I don't have powers, I don't have a secret special mission. There is no bad guy in this scenario, no secret plot. I don't have those kinds of skills or instructions or the desire to use them even if I did. Anyhow drop-off would have come before now, even if I somehow had told them we didn't need it, protocol would be to deliver supplies anyway. All this is that's happening to us is just happening, and it's not my fault."

"Whose fault is it then?"

Maddie realised she was moving the knife back and forth, in both hands, under the table. She had been grinding the blade between her legs into the hard plastic of the chair, cutting a long groove into it.

"Maddie, I think you have seriously gone off the deep end," Charles said, softly. "I think you need to…" He sucked a breath in through his teeth. "You need a solid fuck, honestly. You need to get yourself all scraped raw and start over. I'm not the man to do it. I don't know, man, woman, arm-length dildo?"

"What is the question I should have asked?" Maddie said, slowly. "If none of this is right?" Her eyes hurt; she wasn't blinking, the crack in her iris was widening, letting the dark pour in from her pupil. It stung; a blurry patch had appeared in the air, soon it would blind her. Charles seemed taken aback at her whole face. She took one hand off the knife and patted the skin under her eyes.

"Am I – the I is *you*, Maddie, in this situation – am I going to kill Charles? That's the question you should have asked yourself, Maddie. And why do I want to kill Charles so bad? And – who else have I killed? It's getting to be pretty sparse in here – and what else might I have done, thinking I was in my right mind to do it? Questions plural that you need to ask yourself and that we might need to hear an answer to."

"I hate you," said Maddie. "Even when you think you are talking me down off the ledge you are demeaning me."

"I wasn't thinking about ledges. We're right down at the bottom, here."

"Oh, very good. Good flourish. Don't think you can confuse me as easily as all that. I have a firmer grip than you could ever suppose."

"Clearly," said Charles.

"Tell me what you did, Charles. Tell me which of them you… hurt, you killed. I might have got the details wrong. Tell me if you know if anyone's coming to save us after the experiment's run through."

"No," said Charles. He leaned forward and snatched the knife from Maddie's hand and lunged at her. Maddie buckled and knocked over her chair, righted herself, stood, grabbed the knife and threw herself backwards across the floor. Charles pushed forward and back; Maddie yelled in anger. She tried to headbutt him and hurt herself, the knife fell to the floor in a clatter, and in shock Maddie rubbed her forehead. Blur in her eye. Charles groping about on the floor when Maddie kicked him in the ribs. The others in the room stood up, and they were saying hey hey hey now, like tuneless backing singers, and she could almost laugh.

"Oh come on," said Maddie. "We all know he should be thrown in the fucking cells."

"Cells?" said Charles. "Oh my God, Maddie."

He looked so reasonable that Maddie stopped for a moment. And that was when he made another feint and got the knife, rose, and stabbed it in at her side, right where the waist came in. Butter knife though it was, in up to the hilt. Maddie screamed bitterly and pulled the knife out of her flesh and brandished it at everyone gathering in, closing in upon her.

"Don't, don't. Do not."

"Hello?" said Beaumont, appearing at the door, looking at the scene coolly. "You've knocked over the card table there."

There was a pause for comprehension.

"Yes, I think I did, when I was getting up," said Maddie. "Sorry for waking you."

"Mm," said Beaumont. "You're bleeding. Let's put a stop to that quick."

When Maddie looked around her, she saw that Etan had moved over to Charles. He had his hand on his shoulder. Edward was pulling Maddie back, gently, and Beaumont was guiding her away. Edward had got the knife away from her, he was holding it at his side. Her hands felt naked, clammy.

Later, Maddie would think about the look Edward and Etan had exchanged, earlier, during the break between games. She hadn't been fully paying attention, and naturally a moment can pass in that gap, a moment with meaning come clear only later on. She had tried always to notice this sort of communication, small though it might be, but in this case, she had failed. Her mind on other things. She had succeeded in another way, all she had had to be all along, and that was to be more convincing than Charles.

The men had made a silent judgement of their own, and now they acted: Etan had Charles' arms pinned back. Edward stepped forward and plunged the butter knife into Charles' throat, and pulled it out again. Both men, the stabber and the stabbed, made a kind of cry. Something wet spurted against Maddie's chest; she backed up. Later she would understand it, but just then the noises – guttural, bellowing – and the pain in her side had each been unbearable. Beaumont had helped her to the sink. They pressed at the wound with a cloth while pulling out surgical thread from a small white box. Beaumont was being a little rough with her, distracted, as though someone important was coming soon and Maddie needed to be patched up before then, to look her best, so the visitor would not be affronted. For a second, Maddie's mother's face floated before her, some instance in childhood when she had cleaned up Maddie's scuffed knee and told her it would be better soon, and kissed the plaster before applying it, for luck. The memory fell away into the current reality of blood and the halt, loud gurgling sounds from the other side of the room.

"Did he do any of it?" Maddie was saying. She must have said it more than once, she thought. She was sure she had said it more than once. But no one was answering her, and it was very important that she should know. Beaumont offered no words of comfort.

"Eloise is dead." Etan had re-appeared. He talked without emotion. "Her nightgown was all out of place. I sorted it. She looks okay now."

"Well," said Maddie. "Dorothy-Ann's dead too." The room looked very large and the people remaining in it did not look at her. All the tables had been cleared to one side. Edward was mopping the red off the grey floor, alongside Kaspar, who was on his hands and knees with a scrubbing brush.

"I suppose things will look up from here," Kaspar said. "When a situation is open-ended and you find this stressful, settling on one definitive answer, regardless of whether it is authoritative, can help improve your wellbeing. Another choice is if you can have stoic response to the undefined, knowing you yourself are responsible for your reaction to the pains of the living world."

"I think that works," said Beaumont. "I would try to make it sound more natural. It is a little textbooky. Harder to get behind the sentiment, in that form."

"That's a lot of words, Kaspar," said Etan. Edward simply looked at the floor. The blood was very dilute at that point. One more bucket, and it would do.

It took a long time for the effects of that night to lessen and for Maddie to get out of her bed without calling out from the pain. Her eye had been blurry for a few days, then vision restored itself without intervention to a reasonable degree. She no longer had any questions fit to speak of, even to herself. She went to the pantry when she felt like it, as infrequently as possible. No one was keeping a record of rations. On the somethingth of the fourteenth month, she noted the total absence of solid protein, vegan or otherwise. All the food for the mice had been eaten, and then the mice, though Maddie had locked herself in the showers when that was happening. She couldn't remember her last hot meal. Even the thought of 'hot meals' sounded unlikely; all that came to mind was a hot porridge of ingredients – lentils, foamy dust-specked bouillon and dehydrated carrot pieces, rehydrated – which once long ago she and some others had clawed out from under a manic wreckage. It lingered there in her mind, that hot meal, steaming creepily. There was still plenty of powdered milk left. She had tried at first to pretend it was derived from something mineral, like chalk, but now she did not care and had given herself over to the process of preparing and consuming it. She made herself up a cup with barely enough water to make it fluid, moved through into the common room and stood at the windows, holding her spoon to the glass.

"Another beautiful day," she said, white grit in her teeth.

No one had touched the playing cards since the last poker game; they had been swept to one side with a mop during the cleaning. Maddie noticed them every day. Every day she came in and wondered who might have decided to go in the night, and if they had achieved their end calmly and without mess, as Etan had, just a day after the poker game. One day, only she and Kaspar remained. She had thought Beaumont might outlive her, troubled so little, it seemed, by the worst of recent events. But no, Beaumont had died. She wasn't sure how. Their body was still quite heavy as she and Kaspar dragged it to the chapel. It might have been starvation anyway, the effects of malnutrition shutting down the organs. But she wasn't that kind of doctor, and could not in good conscience definitively say.

"Kaspar, could you help me pick these up?"

"The cards? All right."

"I'm afraid they're pretty dirty. They might still be – damp."

"Don't worry about it, I'm used to dirty things."

"Kaspar, you're always so upbeat. But I wonder what kind of qualities Beaumont left you that were just Beaumont's. I feel like you – oh well, don't mind me. It does and it doesn't matter."

"Okay, Maddie."

Kaspar handed her the cards. They were crispy and had distinct brown stains on them marking the backs. It would never again be possible to play a game with them, not if you knew which card each was which beforehand. After she shuffled them into suits, Maddie stood with the cards at the common room window, facing out. It was then that a long something came into the view cut out of the ocean by the base's floodlights: Maddie peered at it, impatient, until it came undulating closer. It was, as far as she could make out, three long, long strips of ominous reddish fabric, matte, a little like a worn curtain, fluttering ragged along the length of the trench, or at least for the length of the trench as far as could be seen from the base windows. She could see no top to it, even when she pressed herself against the thick distorting glass. Each strip was perhaps half a metre wide, and endlessly tall and moving through the water very slowly, as if dragged by a boat high above. Two miles above. Maddie thought of all the things in creation it could feasibly be, and then remembered footage of a giant jellyfish she had seen online – that her partner had shown her, just as she was first trying to make up her mind whether to take up this position, back when she hadn't even been called for the second interview yet. In the video, the giant jellyfish was mostly drifting, tangling up in the darkish, matte, slickering length of its arms and untangling itself as it floated by. Stygiomedusa gigantea, that was its name, and it was that colour as camouflage, reddish-brown so that it would not reflect even the meagrest light available down below. Twelve or so metres long, typically – this specimen was far, far larger, at least from her limited perspective. Her partner had been trying to horrify her then with evidence of the unknown hideousness of the depths. Look at this, look where you will be living. How perverse to take up home where these kind of creatures dwell. Maddie had been unmoved. At least, most of her had not been frightened.

And now here came the length of the stygiomedusa, its mushroom-shaped head far up out of sight. Its flat, fluttering arms moved twisting through that sliver of light the base created and maintained. And then, as Maddie watched, the creature drifted out of the range of the light, and into the darkness again.

She had some tasks to do for the day: she moved away from the window and with a languid, exhausted walk crossed the room into the kitchen section, and stood there breathing deeply through her nose. She could smell the residue of the cannabis oil droplets, though Kaspar had scrubbed all surfaces clean – he continued to do so daily, though the only mess that was ever made came from the person of Maddie, who was despite her frugal habits now, prone to occasionally moving a chair out of place. With few other distractions, Kaspar had become overly fastidious in behaviour, and that suited her just fine. She had taken up regular and careful washing of her side since the bandages had come off, more than she ever had in her life touched that place on her body, to keep the wound from festering. They would be orderly together. Maddie thought she might have a joint later; it had been a while since the last one. There were plenty of buds left in the grow room, pegged and dried out on a wire under the seedtray table. For now though, she went to her office, switching the sign to occupied, as she always did.

She sat on the sofa, looking at her file. Her file was the only one that remained safe from storage and recycling. She looked at first at the very basic, essential facts. The type of medications she took (birth control, vitamins, nothing else), her height and weight on pre-entry to the base. Some notes from a third party psychologist, describing her as 'reliably dedicated to her work', like a lazy teacher on a school report. Under incidences, which had long been blank, she had dutifully recorded her outburst at the poker table and written that it was recommended that other members of the crew take over her psychology shift permanently. In her 'constants', blank as always in the beginning, she began to write.

Madeleine is…Madeleine is tired.

She had written 'Madeleine is tired' many times. It was nothing new. It was most often a challenge to herself, asking her to push past this unilluminating phrasing towards some new insight into her psyche, to make sure, by posing such an obvious, easy line that she did not shrug off the necessary work before it had even begun. But now her fingers on the touchscreen were bones beneath a white skin made of powdered milk. Her hair was long and fell out when she ran her hands through it. The lights flickered a second, or her vision did. She looked up; there was nothing to look up at, just a desk, a grey wall, a few of the crew's old posters she had put up. Dorothy-Ann's postcard of the Trinity College Library, Etan's photograph of himself and his mother, taken when he was a child. The base was silent in its usual humming way. She moved her file towards the recycle bin without backing it up, and clicked to empty. Then she walked to the chapel to look at the crew.

For the length of time some of them had been in there, it was surprising how little of a smell there was. If anything was detectable it was the smell of something church-like that did not belong in the chapel at all, smell of incense and cold stone and the moisture the comes off the holy water troughs, or whatever they were called. A smell of something old and stable, of spaces that are so thickly-walled they seem subterranean, but are not. Their own special sort of encasements of time and the many varieties of the human desire not to be alone. Maddie entered the room and walked down the aisle to the stained glass window; it lit up automatically. It was about as tall as she was and composed of red, orange, yellow, purple, pink and green shards of colour, with false black lead striping between each piece, and a light-box behind it providing the glow. The colour that appealed the most was the green, the rarest piece, repeated only three times in the abstract design. Green was Maddie's favourite colour. She inspected the light-box and found that it was hung against the wall on simple hooks and did not appear to be connected to the main power supply – it must run on a battery, which made sense for how little energy it required. It wasn't a strong light, less than forty watts, not enough to read by. She thought then that if the base's power generation system failed, this, among some other small appliances and emergency lanterns, would be one of the only sources of illumination. It was warm, not hot to the touch; she found herself leaning into it, pressing her scrawny body against the smooth false glass. With her eyes closed she could still see the colours swirling together.

One day, Maddie thought, lacking regular upkeep the generator would fail, and after a time there would be no one to trip the stained glass light. Then there would be no colours glowing in these rooms because there would be no one to want to see them, or because there was no one to see them, depending on how one thought of it. And by then almost all of the visible light would be absent from the base, the only thing would be darkness. Maddie was not sure if colour could exist in the dark, if there was something inherent in colour that kept it itself, even without the spectrum of light reaching it. She wondered, briefly, if the stained glass window had been installed to give rise to such questions so that a visitor to the chapel might infer from it some subtle aspect of the divine.

"No, no," she said to the room. "No."

But her words settled nothing, because she knew so little, and because there was no one now to look to for the verifiable facts, nor to be with for the considered, or flippant, or rough airing of opinion. She opened her eyes, and still leaning in as much as she could to the surface of the glass, tapped each of the three green shards with the tips of her fingers. It had a touch of blue in it, she thought. Like thick, new leaves on low-growing plants. It was rare, and she was seeing it.

Maddie pulled herself away, went and lit her joint with the offering candle lighter. She kneeled down at a pew on the side opposite the bodies, and blew a cloud of smoke into the chapel air. Yes, one day it would be completely dark in here. But that is how it was, she thought, before us.

A long time ago she and the rest of them must have sailed down to the newly-installed base through the layers of the water, headlights shining, revealing the way. There must have been a launch day, day zero, when they said goodbye to those who had come to see them off, with tight hugs and hurried whispers, the final touches, touching fingers, the parting, the space between the leavers and the left increasing. But now there was nothing, no space to speak of, because the distance was too great for her to understand. She came to herself and looked at the sheet-wrapped bodies stacked between the pews and the wall. She stubbed out the joint and walked to the doorway, staring into the room a moment longer, at the stained glass, then closed the door. The coloured lights hovered in her vision a moment longer, colouring the hallway, then faded out slowly.

She walked back to the window of the common room. The sounds of Kaspar hoovering the metal baseboards echoed from another room. We all die alone, that was the stereotype, but sometimes we all die together in one safe place. Kaspar would run down eventually, after the generators stalled out, succumbing to some small electrical issue or another. She sat on a table and put her thin arms gently around her knees and closed her eyes, talking herself through the details of the stygi-omedusa. All the details that were known of the rarely-seen creature, and how it related to other animals in its genus. And from there she moved down other branches of the tree of life, the part she had studied at any rate, as they occurred to her, her lips moving as she recalled one species and another. Maddie thought about her heart, burning as it beat, or pulsing like a creature moving through the dark. Her side felt stiff; she placed one hand on it, breathing in and shuddering out. The sounds of hoovering rose and fell. She rested her head on her knees and the sound of her heart came rushing loud in her ears, back and forth, blood rushing and life circling, a heart that might, if she believed it, be lighting up and falling back into the darkness inside her chest. She supposed her heart would fail some time soon, as it always was meant to. Beyond the window of the common room the lights lit up the trench for a few metres, and in that space a fine grey snow was falling, steady and unceasing.

ACKNOWLEDGEMENTS

This book owes boundless thanks to: my parents Patricia and Colin McClory (particularly thanks to my dad for his prompt on the superb lyrebird, a replacement for the one he did not see, for 'The Beautiful Birds of the Aftermath'), to Douglas Dunbar for his endless and generous support, to the brilliant women of 404 Ink – Heather McDaid and Laura Jones – for publishing it, to Robbie Guillory for editing it. To team PhD, to Jenny Brown, to the editors of literary journals who have kindly put out my stories into the world, for all the selfless work editors do, with such care and attention always. To all of you who've read and supported my writing. A charm for you all, whatever your days have for you ahead.

ABOUT HELEN MCCLORY

Photo: Sinead Grainger

Helen McClory lives in Edinburgh and grew up between there and the Isle of Skye. Her debut novel, *Flesh of the Peach*, was published by Freight in Spring 2017. Her first collection, *On the Edges of Vision*, won the Saltire First Book of the Year 2015 and was republished by 404 Ink in Spring 2018. There is a moor and a cold sea in her heart.

ON THE EDGES OF VISION

by Helen McClory

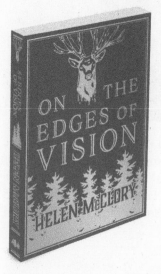

In Helen McClory's award-winning debut short story collection *On the Edges of Vision*, unease sounds itself in the language of legend. Images call on memory, on the monstrous self. The skin prickles against sweeps of light or darkness, the fantastic or the frightful; deep water, dark woods, or scattered flesh in desert sand.

Whether telling of a boy cyclops or a pretty dead girl, drowned sailors or the devil himself, each story draws the reader towards not bleakness but a tale half-told, a truth half-true: that the monster is human, and only wants to reach out and take you by the hand.

WINNER: Saltire Society First Book of the Year, 2015

Available from 404 Ink: 404ink.com/shop